I0669016

# Ruff Justice

## by

## Tara Choate

*A Canine Accounting Caper*

Copyright Notice

This is a work of fiction. Names, characters, places, and incidents are either the product of the author's imagination or are used fictitiously, and any resemblance to actual persons living or dead, business establishments, events, or locales, is entirely coincidental.

**Ruff Justice**

COPYRIGHT © 2025 by Tara Choate

All rights reserved. No part of this book may be used or reproduced in any manner whatsoever including the purpose of training artificial intelligence technologies in accordance with Article 4(3) of the Digital Single Market Directive 2019/790, The Wild Rose Press expressly reserves this work from the text and data mining exception. Only brief quotations embodied in critical articles or reviews may be allowed. Contact Information: info@thewildrosepress.com

Cover Art by *Tina Lynn Stout*

The Wild Rose Press, Inc.
PO Box 708
Adams Basin, NY 14410-0708
Visit us at www.thewildrosepress.com

Publishing History
First Edition, 2026
Trade Paperback Print ISBN 978-1-5092-6434-6
Digital ISBN 978-1-5092-6435-3

*A Canine Accounting Caper*
Published in the United States of America

## Dedication

To all the dogs I've loved before.

Chapter 1

*It must be a full moon.*

Irene Lisner answered the knock on her front door to find her sister's husband. Her sister, Angie, and her husband, Jason, lived and worked in Wilsonville, thirty minutes north of her house in Salem, Oregon. There was no reason Jason should be at her house.

Confused, she cautiously said, "Hi, Jason."

"Hey, Irene. Got a minute?"

"If you don't mind me getting ready for work while we chat."

He shrugged. "No big."

She gestured to the kitchen counter. "Get yourself a cup of coffee." She resumed putting together her lunch. "What's up, Jason?"

He poured himself a mug of coffee, then reached into her refrigerator for milk. "I was in the area. Thought you might want to talk." He stopped, then tacked on, "How's your job going?"

Irene couldn't remember a time when she and her brother-in-law had "talked." Except in the presence of her sister and nephews at family gatherings, she doubted they had exchanged so much as weather information.

She looked at her watch pointedly. "Okay. How's yours?"

He grunted.

Silence stretched out.

She finished packing her lunch and put it in her backpack. "I have two minutes before I have to leave. Either tell me what's on your mind or I'll leave you to enjoy your coffee. Lock up when you leave."

Another moment passed. Irene slung her backpack over her shoulder.

"Why can't she cut me some slack?" Jason muttered. "I'd be a manager, too, if she wasn't always making me stay with the kids."

Jason and Angie both worked for a car sales conglomerate that operated in about a dozen states in the western part of the United States, though they did not work together at the same dealership. Angie had taken a management-level job a several months ago. Jason had stayed on the sales floor. Irene had thought this arrangement was what they wanted.

"Are you wanting out of sales?" she asked.

"This isn't what we agreed to when we moved down here," he stated angrily. "When we left Alaska, she said she wanted to be more stable. I never thought it would be like this."

She set her backpack on the counter. "Be like what?"

He shrugged. "Home all the time. On a budget. On a schedule."

Irene searched for something to say. "Angie counts on you to help with the kids."

He crossed his arms, glared out the window. "But when I'm with the kids, I don't make money. And the day shift is the pits for commissions."

She glanced at her watch. "Jason, you need to talk to Angie—"

Throwing his hands wide, Jason knocked several

pencils out of a mug on the counter. "I do talk to her, but she doesn't care." He leaned down to pick up the pencils.

Irene noticed he missed one. "Jason, it's clear you are upset, but I'm not sure what I can do. You need to talk to Angie. You know I'm the last one she'd listen to."

"She listens to you. It's me she doesn't pay attention to."

Irene studied him. Jason had swept her sister off her feet ten years ago and had kept her enchanted ever since. Blond, tall, and good looking, he normally exuded the confidence of a professional athlete, physical and carefree. Currently, his attractive features were arranged in a sullen expression that had taken over in the last few months. She had noticed friction between Angie and him, but she hadn't thought anything about it. All relationships have rough spots.

"Jason, I have to get to work."

"I know. I shouldn't have come."

Irene's phone started ringing in her bag. It was *Mi Vida Loca*, her sister's ring tone. She ignored it, grabbing her coat. "Stay as long as you need and lock up when you leave."

He agreed. "Hey, I don't see Percy?"

Irene gave him a look of disbelief. "Percy died three months ago."

"Oh. Sorry. I forgot. He was a good old boy."

Enunciating each word, she said, "Yes, he was."

And she shut the door behind her.

****

Even with the interruption, Irene arrived at the state office building in Salem minutes before she was due to start her day. Blocking her entry into the building was a crashed personal vehicle, six police cruisers, and a gaggle of onlookers.

*It really must be a full moon.*

She spotted her friend and office mate, Peter Hampton, among the crowd and walked over. "What happened?" she asked him.

"I don't know," he replied, excited. "They have the whole complex blocked off."

Mishel, the office assistant for their work group, cut in. "They're worried about a terrorist threat."

Irene's boss, John Fisher, joined them. "The guy who crashed the car into the building was arrested, then taken off for DUI and Reckless Driving. The police want to make sure it wasn't some sort of attack before they clear us all to get in."

"Do you think they'll check for structural damages?" Irene asked, watching with the rest of the crowd as a tow truck pulled to the curb and began backing up to remove the crashed vehicle.

John shrugged. "I think the barriers stopped the car before it hit the building."

The gaggle of onlookers watched as the car, rear bumper covered in stickers expounding various conspiracy theories, was peeled away from the concrete pillars that served the dual purpose of marking the main entrance and protecting it from such a ramming.

A uniformed state police officer came out and raised his hands. The crowd turned toward him, straining to hear his announcement. "Thanks for your patience. You can all return to work."

While exciting, the incident also had the effect of ruining the morning schedule. Irene and her coworkers climbed the stairs to their offices with John telling them to be ready for the weekly recap in five minutes.

Five minutes later, cradling her large coffee cup, Irene took her chair in the large conference room of the Oregon Office of Adjudication. The OA was the State of Oregon's answer to the federal Department of Justice. Broadly speaking, the OA provided legal and judicial services to the state of Oregon. The Attorney General led the division, with tasks ranging from child support to consumer protection, which fell under the broad guidelines of a charter. Irene had joined a small division that worked with charities and other nonprofits to enforce laws. As a certified forensic accountant, she often developed evidence for trials, as well as testified as an expert witness for the state if and when charges were brought.

The rest of the investigators filed into the room. Candace Fernandez took the seat next to Irene and they exchanged hellos. John scowled at them all, studying his watch. John hated to be off schedule. "Let's get started."

After the group ran through their list of investigations and gave update reports, John assigned new cases as necessary. Irene was one of three senior investigators. They had nine junior investigators to do the majority of the required background work. Six office staff served various other functions around the office.

Nearing the bottom of the case files, John shifted his attention to Candace, one of the other senior investigators. "What is going on with the Fallbrook investigation?"

"I haven't had a chance to start," Candace admitted. "I've been finishing up the reports on several other cases."

Irene watched with disbelief and exasperation. Candace Fernandez was the most careful and meticulous of investigators. When Irene had a few weeks to spare on a report, she didn't hesitate to ask Candace to look it over. Candace would spot any discrepancies, typos, or mistakes. But Irene rarely had a few weeks to spare. The unit was fast-paced, often working cases that came under intense public and/or media scrutiny.

Candace's strength was also her weakness. She simply could not meet deadlines; every report needed one more detail checked, or comma inserted. Equally problematic, Candace found it difficult to start a new project. When assigned a case, she spent weeks researching statutes and similar cases before beginning the investigation. Irene knew John compensated for her habits by assigning her fewer projects than the other two senior investigators.

John frowned at her. "You've had the assignment for three weeks."

She shrugged. "I know. I'm sorry. It's been busy."

"Candace, this needs to be resolved. The county commissioners have called me twice to ask for results. They are trying to determine how to handle the lawsuits." He turned to Irene. "Do you have time to assist in getting this closed?"

Irene glanced at Candace. The other woman wore a stiff smile which Irene read as humiliation. "I can do that."

Candace shrugged. "I'll send my notes."
****

Hours later, Irene was in a dour mood. Candace had struggled to find a time to meet and discuss the case. She wanted to meet with her, Irene was assured over and over, but she was so busy. Irene had reviewed the case file on the server, finding it thin and cursory. This led to more excuses. Candace had finally accepted a meeting request, but had made it clear the meeting could only take a half an hour due to a need to meet her carpool.

Five minutes after the appointed time, Candace entered the small conference room where Irene was waiting. "Sorry I'm late. I had a phone call."

Irene attempted to keep unkind thoughts at bay. The entire office had listened to Candace's phone calls from her children. "It's okay. Catch me up. Where is Fallbrook?"

"It's up in the eastern part of Clackamas County, in the unincorporated part of the foothills. The school was decommissioned, then reopened as a charter school."

"Is it all ages and grades?" Irene asked, pleased to have more information, even if it wasn't in the file.

"No. It's a K-8. Older kids bus to the neighboring town of Estacada."

Irene made a note on her ever-present legal pad. "I understand you spoke with the county attorney and education commissioner. They are the ones requesting the investigation?"

Candace twirled her pen. "Yeah. They wanted to lay out the situation." She offered another shrug. "The business manager was fired by the principal. She alleges it was retaliatory because, she says, the school isn't using proper purchasing procedures, and she was about to report it. She's filed a claim for wrongful termination. And in the ensuing kerfuffle, there has been a discrepancy in the reports on student attendance."

Irene signaled with her hand that Candace should continue the explanation.

"According to the county folks, the principal, Gene Schuster, is key to the school's operations. The school has some history. As I said, it's in rural Clackamas County. Back in the fifties, they thought the area was going to expand and they put in a school, but a city never emerged around it. The school survived until the nineteen nineties when the property tax cuts started to dig in. The county decided to close it, but Gene and a community group stepped in with a plan for a charter school. The school has done remarkably well. Gene knows the community, and he's passionate about rural agriculture education."

Irene continued to listen, occasionally making notes.

"Enter Phyllis Dixon," continued Candace, "who's been at the school for a couple of years as the business manager. Apparently, it wasn't a good fit. She and Gene clashed. He fired her."

Irene thought about this for a moment. "I'm assuming you have explained to everyone involved that we don't investigate wrongful termination."

Candace pointed to a line on her notes. "I've spoken to the state business liaison about the terminations. They are investigating and agreed to pass on anything relevant to the reimbursements or attendance. I also spoke to education about what should be done about the discrepancies in attendance."

"What do you see as the next steps?" Irene asked her.

"I've advised the county folks to simply let the wrongful termination suit move forward." Candace shrugged. "I've heard the details. I don't think it will be successful. The county should let the complaint play out rather than try to prevent it."

"What about the attendance reporting?"

"I'd like to take a look at it, because funding is

attached to enrollment."

Irene bobbed her head in agreement. "What about the reimbursements?"

"That's where we focus," Candace said. She handed over a printed spreadsheet. "I did a quick review of the last three years. In that time, Gene has received over fifty-five thousand dollars as reimbursement from the school's accounts."

Irene scanned the information and widened her eyes. "That's quite an amount for reimbursements."

Candace nodded. "I've been doing some research on how charter schools work, trying to understand what I—we—should focus on. Are you familiar with them?"

Irene shook her head.

Candace flipped a page in the legal pad at her side and began reading from her notes. "Fallbrook is a charter school that operates under a contract with the Clackamas School District. Charter schools have more autonomy over their curriculum, staffing, and budget. They get a certain amount of money per student, and it's the school's job to meet the education targets using those funds."

Irene's phone rang, interrupting the lecture. She looked down and saw her sister's information flash across the screen and carefully clicked the button that would discard the call. "I'm sorry. I thought I had turned it off."

Candace hadn't noticed the interruption. "The unusual thing about Fallbrook is they have a number of income-generating special programs, each registered as its own business. The programs are supposed to be independent from the school, with the profits donated back to the school." She looked down at her notes.

"There's a produce stand and a commercial nursery. They accept contracts to grow particular kinds of plants. It appears the profits have been used to fund notable teams, such as the robotics club, that have done well at the state and even national level. Most of the reimbursements are linked to the resulting trips. Gene had been paying the expenses out of pocket then getting reimbursed."

"Was he running this arrangement by anyone?" Irene asked.

Candace signaled her agreement. "The board knew this was happening, but they didn't think it was a problem."

"Why not?"

"Because, quote, '*It's always been this way.*' " Candace said.

Irene understood. "Have you interviewed the board members?"

"Not yet," Candace admitted. "I've been focused on understanding the charter school regulations."

"When you talked to the Clackamas County folks, did you get a sense of why they wanted us involved? It sounds like an audit would be sufficient."

"Honestly?" Candace waited for Irene to give the go ahead. "They want us to get rid of Gene for them."

Irene's brows rose. "What makes you say that?"

"They told me would be easier if Gene retired."

"Why?"

Candace thought for a moment. "I'm reading through the lines here, but in the current political climate, the county doesn't want to publicly tackle the issues the school stands for."

Irene didn't get it. "Like what?"

"Migrant agricultural workers. Like I said, the school focuses on rural agriculture. The school has made inroads with the nearby Latino community. My sense was that the board is afraid of what might happen if Gene was found guilty of wrongdoing. They want the school, and the area, to stay quiet."

Irene stretched in the chair, then rubbed the back of her neck. "Have you interviewed the principal? This Gene Schuster person?"

Candace shook her head. "I've spoken to him briefly about the next steps. He knows what Phyllis has been saying and that there's an ongoing investigation. But I haven't told him any details."

Irene reviewed her notes. "What about the business manager? Phyllis Dixon? Has she been interviewed?"

Now Candace shifted in her chair. "She's called dozens of times. I spoke with her for a few minutes after the third call and told her we were investigating and would interview her later. She's called twice a day ever since, but I've been ducking her calls."

Hoping her thoughts didn't show on her face, Irene lowered her gaze to her notes. "I'll review the annual audits. We'll set up an interview with Phyllis as soon as possible, then we can visit the school for some field work." She remembered she was assisting, not running, the investigation. "If that's okay with you."

"I was planning to start the interviews this week. My schedule has been full," Candace said defensively.

"I understand," Irene said.

Chapter 2

Candace rushed out of the room to meet her carpool, making vague promises to touch base the next day. Irene spent a few minutes leaving a message on the Fallbrook main line, requesting a call back.

Her sister, Angie, had called five times over the course of the day, with Irene sending each call to voicemail. Irene walked the ten minutes it took to get home, then immediately got into her car to drive to the grocery store.

En route to the store, she drove past one of the state buildings complexes that littered Salem. A flicker of movement caught her eye. There were often Canada geese trolling the sides of the road, foraging through the grass around the various state buildings. They had no respect for traffic, so Irene took her foot off the gas. A brownish-gray streak flew down the ditch at the side of the road, sending the frantic geese off in a screaming flight. Irene swerved to the curb and twisted in her seat to see what the streak had been.

A medium-sized dog, thin and quick, was frantically attempting to herd the geese, alternately lunging then chasing them into new groups. The geese who wanted nothing to do with being corralled, took off, flooding the skies, calling desperately to each other. Irene looked around, hoping that even though the dog was muddy and thin, there would be someone nearby who had let the dog run loose. But there was no one in sight.

Irene was about a hundred feet from the intersection with cars coming from both directions, as well as whizzing by in the nearby crossroad. The cars had slowed because the geese were so thick, but the situation was far from safe. Irene pulled the car over as far as possible.

Irene got out, grimacing because her boots were made for the office, not goose-splattered fields. Her skirt and tights were equally ill-equipped to handle a muddy, stray dog. She grabbed a slip leash from the back of the car and a few dry treats from a can she always kept in the car for emergencies. She stood for a moment, assessing the situation.

The increasingly frenzied dog had moved away from the road and was now darting toward a remaining gaggle of overwrought geese who lingered near a building. Irene thought about getting in the car and trying to move closer, but decided against it when the remaining geese achieved liftoff and the dog paused for a moment to bark at its escaped targets.

Unsure that it would do any good, Irene called, "Hey, pretty one. Come see me."

The dog's head swiveled. Its tail wagged, but within second it was back to furious barking and was loping toward another flock of stragglers on the opposite end of the parking lot.

Attracted by the cacophony, a woman came out of the building. She saw Irene and called, "Need some help?"

"Yes," Irene said gratefully. "It's not my dog, but it's been darting around, chasing geese. I'm afraid it will dart out into the street and get hit by a car."

Her new friend nodded, turned around, called into the building, and within a few moments three additional people came out to help.

The dog streaked toward the open fields down the road where geese were currently landing. The humans couldn't match this dog's speed and agility cross-country, and it was a bad idea to chase a loose dog. Before she could come up with a plan, the dog reversed and began dashing back toward Irene and her deputies. Irene crouched, showing her treats. The helpers mimicked her, all of them making high-pitched soothing noises.

The dog paused to review their actions, wagged its tail some more, then returned to its dash toward Irene. As it came closer, it became apparent that Irene was simply in its path. The dog had no intention of stopping for something as mundane as a treat. A single goose, either hurt in the kerfuffle and unable to fly—or too stupid to know any better—had settled down in the muddy grass about ten feet behind Irene and was oblivious to the manic dog once again making a dash toward him.

Irene made a split-second decision. She saw the dog wasn't wearing a collar, but she also didn't think she would ever get closer to the excited canine. She hoped she could pin it and get the slip leash on. *Please don't let it bite.*

As the dog tried to rush by her, she lunged. Instead of a graceful grab, her boot slid on muck and she and dog collided falling into the muddy glop. The dog urgently struggled underneath her, but Irene was able to slip the leash over the head before it got loose and started for the goose again. As she struggled to stand up in the slippery mud, she took stock.

The dog was at the end of the lead, frantically barking at the goose. The goose appeared unfazed by the dog's intention. Irene held her arms away from her sides. Most of her clothes were covered in grime. The would-be helpers looked astonished.

The original woman asked tentatively, "Are you okay?"

Irene smiled. "Compared to what? But nothing appears broken."

This broke the spell and everyone moved toward her. Someone removed the dog's leash from her hand, trying to control the barking and lunging dog. Another woman steadied Irene as she picked her way out of the mud. "Your clothes," she said mournfully. "I am so sorry."

Irene looked down and then over at the dog. The barking continued. "I admire his stamina," she said dryly. The group giggled nervously.

"I take it that dog doesn't belong to any of you? Or someone around here?"

They all shook their heads.

Irene wiped her hands on her ruined skirt, then brushed mud off her chin. "Okay."

"I guess we should call the shelter?" someone murmured.

There was silence.

Finally, Irene said, "Yes. That's the best thing. If someone is looking for the dog, they'll call there first."

One of the onlookers took out their phone and called the shelter line. Since the shelter worked on an automated system, there was no pickup.

After several tries, Irene interrupted. "Alright. I'm

already ruined for the day. I have a kennel in my car, so I'll load the dog up and drive him over to the shelter. That way it'll be safe and easy to find if anyone is looking for him. It'll probably be faster, anyway, than trying to get through to the shelter and then waiting for them to come here and pick him up." She glanced at her watch. "Even if we could get them to come this late in the day."

The others agreed, so Irene took the leash and thanked the group. The dog bounced along at the end of the leash, continuing to announce his intentions to the geese who were already settling across the street again.

Irene had to pick up the dog to get him into Percy's old kennel, still in the back of her car. *What's a little more mud?* She finally saw that it was an intact male dog. Once she shut the door, the dog quieted down. When she got into the driver's seat, the dog had shifted to sit alertly looking forward, appearing to anticipate a ride.

"Sure, now it's easy." Irene muttered.

The Marion County Dog Shelter was about three miles down the road, on the outskirts of Salem. Once in the parking lot, she got out and entered the door marked, "Strays." Apparently, when she had wiped off her face, she had not done a good job. The attendant gasped when she saw Irene's muddy face and grime-covered clothes. Even in her scrubs, the worker took a step back. She quickly recovered and professionally directed Irene to fill out the paperwork. Irene did so, then went back to the car to get the dog.

While the dog was still panting, its eyes had lost their insane glow. In fact, it met her eyes and gave its tail a soft wag, tongue dripping down to the side, for all the world saying, *Wasn't that awesome?*

Irene smiled. Taking the leash, she let the dog out. He happily bobbed along beside her, investigating each scent on the short walk. Irene smiled again. When they got to the door, the dog stuck his nose into the crack, then gave another *Isn't this fun* look.

The shelter staffer was waiting for her inside the hallway. Her eyes cut between Irene and the equally disheveled dog.

"I had to do a full body tackle to catch him," Irene explained.

The dog looked thrilled with himself.

A smile bloomed across the attendant's face. "Wow. That must have been quite a show."

Irene rolled her eyes.

They transferred the leash, and the attendant gently tugged the leash to get the dog to move with her. He turned and threw Irene a betrayed look. *We were having such good fun.*

Irene couldn't help herself. She crouched down. "You need to stay here. This is the place your people will find you. You'll be safe."

The shelter staff piped up. "Look how thin he is. I think he's going to be a stray." She met Irene's eyes. "Do you want us to give you a call after the three-day hold so you can come get him?"

As Irene turned down the street to her house, she pondered that question but getting out of her dirty clothes was the more pressing matter. The mud was getting dry enough to flake, and while a mud bath might be okay in a spa, this particular treatment smelled too bad to be anything she would willingly endure.

When she got within sight of her house, she saw Angie's SUV in her driveway.

Of course. *More full-moon drama.*

Irene trudged up the steps to see Angie sitting at the kitchen counter, a mug of something at her elbow, working on her phone. She looked up when she heard the door, her mouth opening then closing, her comment frozen by the sight of Irene.

"I'm going to take a shower now," Irene said evenly. "Please."

Twenty minutes later, Irene emerged clean and scrubbed, wearing jeans and a sweater.

Angie was waiting with a cup of coffee. "I thought you might need this."

Irene took it from her and sat down at the counter. After Irene had taken a few sips, Angie said, "Should I ask?"

In slow, measured words, Irene said, "On my way home, there was a stray dog chasing some geese. I ended up more or less tackling it in a muddy field."

"Oh."

Irene took another drink. "Angie, it has been a weird and not terribly easy day. Just tell me why you're here. We'll sort it out and then you can go home."

Angie didn't immediately respond. Finally, she said, "I kind of wanted to talk."

"Is this the same subject that caused Jason to come the house this morning?"

"Jason came by this morning?"

"Yes. In fact, he was still here when I left for work."

"What did he say?'

"Not much. He was agitated. You've been calling me all day. I figured you guys had an argument."

Angie huffed but didn't comment.

"Angie, spit it out." She looked down at her cup, "I

18

may need something stronger."

Angie snorted. "What? Espresso. You don't drink."

"I'm considering taking it up."

"If you're serious, I could use a beer."

Irene didn't drink because it could aggravate her recently diagnosed Multiple Sclerosis, but she kept a few beers in her refrigerator for her family and friends. She handed Angie a beer then crafted a cup of tea. "Tempting, but I'll stick with tea. What's the latest problem?" Irene winced. That had come off harsher than she had intended.

Angie glared. "You make it sound like there's always a problem."

"Oh, for heaven's sake, Angie."

Angie gulped down air, whether to prevent herself snapping back or bracing herself to begin. "Okay. You're right. It's a problem. I just don't... I'm not sure... I can't decide what to do."

"What happened?" Irene said, softening her tone.

"Well, the first thing is that my dealership offered me a position as the General Manager of a high-end Bend dealership."

Irene racked her knowledge of Angie's workplace. Irene thought this would be a promotion, but there were so many managers in car dealerships it was hard to be sure. "That's good, right?" she offered tentatively.

Angie bobbed her head with enthusiasm. "It's the top position. The Bend dealership leads sales in the region."

"Congratulations."

"Well, it's not quite that simple. We'd have to move."

Irene dipped her chin. "That can be expensive."

"Oh, the company will pay for the move."

Irene blinked. "Okay. That's great. And you rent, so you'd only be on the hook for a few months."

"The company says they'll pay any fees associated with terminating the lease."

"Wow. That's generous. Are you worried about the kids?"

Angie thought about that. "Well, I'm not crazy about moving them. The company wants me in Bend within four weeks. And I'd have meetings between now and then."

"That's fast."

"Yeah. When I told Jason about the offer, I suggested that he could stay over here until the end of the school year. With the pay increase, he could even leave his job and we wouldn't be much behind."

Irene listened.

"He freaked out," Angie continued. "He said that I was preventing him from getting into management. He said that I and kids were holding him back from having a career. He said he wanted to move back to Alaska and that we should never have left. He started talking about how I was sabotaging him as a man and how I was working to make sure he wasn't successful."

Irene blinked. "Okay. He didn't take it well."

Angie rolled her eyes. "Then he stormed out. I didn't know he had come down here."

"I'm not sure he meant to. He acted like he wasn't sure what he wanted."

Angie looked down at her glass. "I know he hasn't been as… happy the last few months, but I honestly didn't think he was thinking all that."

"Maybe he isn't," Irene suggested. "Maybe it was

heat of the moment."

Angie looked thoughtful. "He's not the type to come up with all that in the moment. Sure, he gets mad, but it's usually about stuff. Something that happened. Not about intentions and the future and all the rest."

"It sounds like maybe it's been building for a while," Irene said gently.

"Maybe." Angie looked out the window.

Irene waited.

Finally, Angie continued. "I don't want to sound paranoid, but I think there's something else going on."

"Something else?"

"I've wondered about… about him seeing someone else. There hasn't been any working late or that kind of thing. In fact, he's been at home more often lately. Picking up the kids. Taking up slack at home. But he's also been sort of secretive with the computer. And his phone."

"Could he be looking for another job?"

Again, Angie looked down. "It's possible. When he wigged out today, I thought '*Well, okay, this is it. He's gonna come out with it.*' Then he left. I know he's mad, but I'm not sure about what." Angie paused to regain some composure. "When he started to talk about Alaska, I thought he was going to insist we go back there."

"Would you?"

"I don't know. I like being a manager, and I'm excited about the possibility of my own dealership. But I also love him. And the kids. I don't want to have to choose."

"You don't have to choose right now," Irene said. "In fact, you probably shouldn't even try. Sit down and talk. Find out what's going on."

Angie tipped her head, but she lacked confidence. "But Irene, here's the thing. I don't want to go back to Alaska. I like being a manager."

"So you know your bottom line. But my advice, since you asked for it, is to talk to him. You're in a relationship, not a dictatorship. Your career is on the upswing right now, but that doesn't mean that he won't have something awesome soon. Ask him if he wants to go back to having his own business. He enjoyed that. And he was making money. Maybe he needs a new challenge."

Angie pursed her lips. "Maybe."

Irene patted her sister's hand. "I'll listen for as long as necessary, honey, but the fact of the matter is that I can't answer any of these questions. It has to be the two of you."

\*\*\*\*

That night, Irene dreamed that the gray dog rode in a sleigh pulled by Canada geese into an airport. Percy was there, directing traffic from the air control tower. An attractive man that she couldn't quite place brought a hot air balloon shaped like a border collie and sat it down next to the sleigh. Jason and the boys were studying a gigantic map of the South Pole, mounted on a moose, caribou, and elk. The animals were wearing sleigh bells. Angie and her mother were wearing bikinis on the deck of an enormous yacht made up to look like a log cabin. Irene was locked in a glass elevator that wouldn't move, but where she could see everything.

She woke up depressed.

Chapter 3

The next morning, Irene was relieved to complete her morning routine without visitors.

On her way to meet Candace at the state motor pool building, she passed by the field where the skinny gray dog had chased the geese the day before. Currently undisturbed, the geese foraged by the hundreds on the lawns surrounding the state buildings.

Irene thought about the dog. Her response when asked if she would like a call back if he was not claimed had been a lackluster no. The shelter staffer held back a knowing smirk when Irene changed her response a few moments later. Irene explained that she had put in an application to foster a dog after Percy died. The technician told her the application was still good, so Irene agreed to foster the dog if someone didn't claim him.

Irene remembered her dream of the night before, featuring Percy and the gray dog.

Irene supposed Percy's death shouldn't have come as a surprise. He had been at least fifteen. Dog friends had been mentioning his obvious age for quite a while, urging her to get a puppy. She had ignored them. When Percy started walking into things around the house, she had taken him to vet, expecting to be told he had cataracts. The doctor informed her it was a brain tumor. Within a week, Percy started to have seizures. The vet explained the attacks weren't painful, but that they would grow increasingly worse and more frequent. No medication would help. Irene had still denied the reality until Percy's seizures were nearly constant.

His absence made her heart hurt.

At the state motor pool, she discovered Candace had already collected the car, so Irene loaded her backpack and computer, and they were off for Fallbrook.

"How is it being back?" Irene asked.

"Back?" Candace asked, glancing toward her

"Yeah. You were on parental leave until a few weeks ago," Irene clarified.

"Oh." Candace paused. "It's hard. I'm still pumping milk for Summer."

"Let me know if you need a break," Irene offered.

Candace signaled her agreement.

"How are your boys doing with the new baby?" Irene knew Candace had two young boys at home, around two and four years old. Since she'd been hired five years ago, Candace had taken three rounds of parental leave.

"Joe is doing alright. He had his jealousy moment when Zak arrived. Zak is acting out a bit. He's never been as easy as Joe."

Irene groaned in sympathy. "When Mike was born, my sister told me that her son began crying over the least little thing. She thought she'd go nuts."

Candace laughed. "I wish that was all Zak was doing. He's been potty trained for ages. In fact, we waited to get pregnant until he was potty trained because we didn't want to have two children in diapers. But he's started to wet the bed again."

"I'm sorry," Irene said sincerely.

"I'm sure it will work out," Candace said, clearly trying to move past the subject. "One day at a time."

They fell into silence.

Candace interrupted first. "John read me the riot act yesterday."

"That must have been upsetting," Irene murmured.

"I told him there is too much to do, but he got impatient. He said I need to prioritize."

*I agree*, Irene thought, but said, "It's tough to do."

"It feels like the cases come on an assembly line."

"I can see that."

"We never get a minute to figure anything out. It's always 'here's another case'."

Irene was already tired of her role as sympathetic listener, but knew it wasn't the time to give an honest opinion. They had always worked together easily. It wasn't the time to offer an honest opinion. She searched for something to say. "This is a hard business. We don't make too many people happy."

Candace hit the indicator to signal their exit off I-5.

\*\*\*\*

They stopped in Oregon City for a cup of coffee, then drove east into the mountains. The road was narrow and followed the course of the river. Agricultural fields and livestock pens spread out across the landscape. The GPS warned the school would be coming up on the left, so Candace slowed down for the turn.

Fallbrook School bore the generic, unprepossessing look of many of the low-slung schools built in the middle of the last century. The aged building looked to be in good repair, with brightly colored paint and a parking lot free from potholes.

The "strong agricultural focus" was obvious. There

were a great many garden areas and a few grassy fields set aside for sports. The garden areas were already in production, with some traditionally tilled, some covered in crops, and some mulched. Raised garden beds popped up regularly. Irene saw several consumer-level greenhouses as well as a large, plastic-covered cold frame near the building. More cold frames lined the area along a road. A large poultry house graced the school courtyard, with chickens and ducks sharing the carefully tended yard.

Irene and Candace made their way to the main office. After securing visitors badges, they followed the front office secretary to an office beyond the main work area. At the door, their guide cleared her throat to get the occupant's attention. Hearing the noise, the man looked up. He grimaced, put aside his paperwork, and stood.

Irene had been expecting Gene Schuster to be an aging flower child with ugly, flat shoes and tie-dyed shirt. Instead, the man working behind the desk looked like a modern farmer, with a feed-store gimme cap, thick brown jacket, and well-worn boots. He was of average height and solid. His hair was so short it was impossible to tell its color, but his eyes were brown. Gene looked to be in his early fifties, which surprised Irene. She had been expecting someone in their seventies or eighties to match the description of "around forever".

"Sorry," he said, coming toward them, hand extended. "I lost track of time." Irene and Candace introduced themselves, and they shook hands. Gene gestured for them to sit in chairs across from him. He thanked the office worker and closed the door.

"Thank you for seeing us on such short notice," Irene said.

"No problem. How can I help?" His tone was up-front, and his body language indicated he was prepared.

Irene decided to take him at face value. "As you know, your former business manager, Phyllis Dixon, is making some claims about accounting irregularities."

Gene bobbed his head stiffly.

"The county commissioner contacted the Oregon Office of Adjudication to request assistance in looking into this," Irene continued. "They want to make sure this is thoroughly investigated and cleared up."

Again, Gene nodded. His face was expressionless.

Irene waited for a moment. It was unusual for someone in Gene's situation to not say something at this point. A defensive statement. A careless comment about things having been blown out of proportion. Gene remained still.

Irene looked over at Candace. Candace looked down at her notes.

"Why have you been reimbursed over fifty-five thousand dollars in the last three years?" Irene asked flatly.

"Running a school is expensive," he said calmly. And did not continue.

More silence.

Candace spoke up. "That is an unusually high reimbursement amount. The average for a school of this size and your position is closer to two thousand per year. And for many schools, it's much lower."

"It's an average for a reason," Gene said without concern. He sat in his desk chair, arms resting on the desk surface. "There are highs and there are lows."

Irene studied him. "Do you mind my asking what you did before you went into education?"

His lips twitched. "I was in the army."

"Where did you serve?"

"First Iraq War. Sergent First Class," he added, cutting off her next question.

This was a man used to pressure. Irene decided to stop being subtle. "Why did you fire Ms. Dixon?"

"In my opinion, she was no longer a good fit for this position."

"What changed to make you form that opinion?"

He paused before answering. "I believe she was losing patience with working in education."

"Why was that a problem? Why didn't you let her make a career decision on her own?"

"I did not think it was safe for her to continue to be around the children."

"Why not?"

"She had a physical confrontation with one of the children."

While Irene paused to consider her next question, Candace stepped in with a suggestion. "Maybe we should start at the beginning? Get some basic information before we ask our questions?"

"That's a good idea," Irene agreed.

Gene did not show any relief. "If you brought boots, we can start with a tour of the school."

Sensing Gene would not offer any more, Irene collected her bag. "That would be nice. It will give us context when we review the paperwork."

\*\*\*\*

Irene and Candace changed into more appropriate footwear, then met Gene back in front of the school complex. Gene had asked the vice-principal, Miriam Freeman, to join them on the grounds tour.

Miriam was a tall, thin woman with an ageless bone structure that made her exact age hard to guess. Irene thought she might be in her fifties. Miriam served as the sixth-grade teacher and co-ed soccer coach as well as the vice-principal. Irene quickly understood she had a forthright, vigorous love of the school, students, and program.

"Phyllis Dixon was all about power and dramatics, nothing left over for common sense or compassion," Miriam said, shaking Irene's hand, then Candace's. "If you have any sense, you'll help us put this whole thing behind us and get on with it."

"Let's start with the fields," Gene suggested.

Miriam started marching down a gravel path toward the back of the school grounds. Irene, Candace, and Gene followed. "Fallbrook is a K-8 charter school," she began. "We accept students from outside the area, though many of our students are from this area."

"Can we start at the beginning?" Candace asked, already struggling to match the brisk pace. "What is a charter school?"

Again, Miriam responded, used to the role of instructor. "Laws differ around the country, but in Oregon a charter school can be established through an application that is sponsored by the local school district. The group that puts in the application has to have various things approved before they can even apply."

"What would be the benefit of setting up a charter school as opposed to a private school?" Candace asked.

"A public charter school is eligible for state and federal funding, a private school is not."

"Can the group setting up the charter school—"

"The applicant," Miriam interrupted.

29

"—Can they be a for-profit group?

"No," Gene replied. "The group must be an IRS registered 501(c)(3)."

"The main reason for setting up a charter school," Miriam continued, "is usually to offer a specialized curriculum. For example, tech schools focusing on industrial skills. Prep schools. Advanced musical or language curriculum."

"That's one reason," Gene interjected, stooping to pull a small weed, "but there are schools that have evolved to meet the needs of small, rural communities. Many parents would rather keep their kids close rather than have them bus an hour or more to a larger community."

"Is there a difference between a charter school and an alternative school?" Irene asked.

Miriam indicated she had heard the question but paused before answering. "I hate to do this, but to answer your question, we have to go into vocabulary terms."

Candace and Irene were now following Gene, who had grabbed a hoe and was actively weeding a row of spinach.

"Alternative school has two meanings that are often used interchangeably and somewhat incorrectly. Back in the day," Miriam waved her hand at some distant time in the past, "a kid went to an alternative school if they were in danger of dropping out or had been expelled or in some other way wasn't 'fitting-in'. It was a polite euphemism for a school trying to serve underachieving students."

Irene spotted a weed and stooped to pluck it. She caught Gene's eye. He winked. "Careful," he warned. "We'll recruit you."

Miriam continued. "These days, the term is still in use and tends to refer to schools trying to serve a small portion of the older student population. Terms like alternative classroom or the school-within-a-school model. Magnet schools are another topic, with the goal there being to offer an intense curriculum in a particular subject."

"So, you're a magnet school?" Candace asked. While the group's pace had slowed, she was still breathing quickly.

Gene shook his head and stood up from his inspection of the crop. "No. Or at least that isn't our intention." He pushed aside thriving rhubarb leaves to let them through. "I was principal of this school when the school district slated it for closure. The cost of keeping up the facility was prohibitive. A group of parents weren't happy about the decision and were vocal about it. I approached them, and we came up with a business plan."

Still panting, Candace interrupted. "I'm confused. Isn't the school a non-profit?"

Gene walked toward a group of picnic tables. Candace collapsed onto one.

Gene sat on one of the benches as well, but almost immediately stood and began picking up and binning the tools, plastic pots, and bits of plastic that were scattered nearby. "The school is run by a non-profit named Fallbrook Agricultural School and Teaching. Obviously, we call it FAST. However, we have several small businesses that operate on a profit, then donate money back to the school. Older kids who are so inclined can use the businesses as part of their study."

"Doesn't that break child labor laws?" Irene wanted

to know.

"No," Gene said flatly. "Children under twelve can work in an agricultural job with parental consent. Children over twelve can get paid. Children over fourteen can do more advanced jobs."

"We have strict age guidelines for work," Miriam assured them. "The kindergarteners plant and maintain the color-wheel flower bed at the front of the school. They learn colors. They make labels for the plants. In warm weather, teachers may do music and stories in the garden. On the other hand, the eighth graders are challenged to plan, create, grow, and maintain their own ten-by-ten garden. The child with the most produce, by pound, is the winner."

"Wouldn't that depend on luck?" Candace asked. "Or what was grown?"

"Yes," Miriam replied with enthusiasm. "But we let the kids make the decisions. If they don't take it seriously, there are consequences. If they pick late-ripening species, that will have an effect. The kids can get amazingly creative with ways to grow the crops vertically or around things."

Having tidied the area, Gene returned to the picnic benches. "So, to return to the original question, some local parents, a few teachers, and I came up with a plan to form the charter and fund it with a combination of state funds and donations. From the beginning, we all wanted an agricultural focus for the school. I had personally seen too many children diagnosed with ADHD that I felt could have been helped by less classroom time and more outdoor exposure."

"But we try to recognize each child as an individual," Miriam broke in. "Not all the children are gardening fiends. If someone wants to read a book instead of research crop rotation, our program can handle that."

During Miriam's explanation, Gene had found a pair of shears and started pruning the hedges surrounding their tables. A student came over and started speaking to Gene in animated Spanish. Gene followed the student toward a large cold frame structure.

Miriam heaved herself up. "Break's over."

They followed Gene into the warm, moist environment of the building. It was packed with vegetation. Irene was not a gardener, but she identified several rows of ferns alongside other greenery.

A group of children Irene judged to be around ten, including the boy who had stopped to talk to Gene, were carefully de-potting ferns. They were supervised by two adults. Beside each student was a notebook with drawings. Irene saw several of the pupils adding sketches and notes to their tablet. A girl waved to them. The kids looked up and the air was flooded with "Hello" and "*Hola*".

Gene was leaning over the original boy's notebook and gesturing from the notebook to the plant. Irene's Spanish wasn't good enough to catch the entire exchange, but she understood Gene was praising the detail and inquiring about class enjoyment. The boy chattered back vigorously.

Another boy came over with a plant and pointed out an insect hiding among the foliage. Intense concentration and discussion followed. The language had shifted back to English, so Irene followed along as the small group discussed what kind of bug it was and if it was likely helpful or harmful.

The interlude lasted around five minutes. Gene interacted with a few more children by name, then indicated to Irene and her group to follow him out of the area. "That's our fourth-grade group," he explained as they moved on. "They are in charge of that fern cluster. They are potting them into big containers this week, but it's slow because they have to do drawings and experiments about the process."

Irene ducked beneath a hanging plant. "How many plants do they manage?"

Gene thought about it. "Fourth grade has eighteen students with one hundred plants between them. I leave it up to the teachers if they want to assign specific plants, but they try hard to make sure each child does the same amount of work."

"Around five plants per student?" Irene confirmed. "That's all?"

"It's more than you think," Miriam said. "At the fourth-grade level, they have to cover multiplication, division, fractions, and geometry for math. It's a key age for language skills, and they are starting to present oral presentations and group projects. Social studies, science, and the arts are also worked into the curriculum. The plants enhance several of these objectives, but kids need the time and space to soak it all in. They aren't field hands."

Irene smiled. "I wasn't complaining. I was worried that the kids had a huge list of chores to get done."

"They have chores," Gene said, his lips twitching to avoid a smile. "Part of growing up is learning you have to get things done. But I think we do a good job of keeping them on the right side of a chain gang."

Irene smiled. "Probably for the best, but it sounds

like an intense workload. Surely it would be easier to open a charter school with a different focus. Why are you working on this?"

Gene frowned at her.

Irene waited.

"Someone needs to teach the next generation of farmers," Gene answered.

\*\*\*\*

Gene and Miriam continued the tour, pointing out other features: a small herd of tiny Shetland sheep; an array of rabbit hutches; pop-up tents for selling produce; tractors; piles of tools. Anything that could be dangerous was carefully locked away, including a small supply of herbicides and pest control.

They paused at the intersection of several paths. Irene could hear Candace gasping for air. Gene gestured to the gardens. "When we started the Produce NOW program, we started small. We constructed these gardens and elected to work on cold weather foods that would take advantage of the time when the kids would be in school."

Miriam continued, "But we were able to expand into summer produce because of a high demand for summer school. The children of the migrant agricultural workers tend to miss school in order to work, particularly in the spring and fall. During the summer, they can come back and make up for some of the things they missed. That has allowed Fallbrook to have a booth at a couple of local farmer's markets."

"We focus on agricultural education as a canvas for learning," Gene expounded. "And a big part of agriculture is making money. The school holds several businesses, each run by a board of directors. Those businesses hold over a dozen products, each with the Fallbrook label. In the upper grades, students are required to work on one of the projects and their work is tied into learning objectives. Younger children assist as part of their overall learning objectives."

Miriam jumped in again. "Most of what's out here are weekend ranchers or industrial farms. Not many young families, except for migrant workers. But we're starting to see younger farmers move into the smaller, older farms. They want to use modern methods, such as organic certification and permaculture to start their business."

Panting slightly, Candace emerged behind the group, grappling with a vine that was clinging to her hair. "Why do you have so many little greenhouses?" She pointed to rows of small, consumer-grade greenhouses. Each had two or three shelves of small plants, covered in thin plastic. The styles of the structures varied, but none looked like they been designed to last.

"We use them to start our grow-to-demand plants."

Irene hadn't heard that term before. "Grow-to-demand?".

Gene explained, "Say a company wants to cut timber. By law, they have to replant the area. They contract someone to produce the seedlings so those seedlings will be available at the right time."

"But it's not only trees," inserted Miriam. "We do ferns, scrubs, and even some grasses. Conservation districts and non-profits need plants to complete their natural restoration plans. They want to find Oregon native plants grown in a habitat similar to where they will ultimately be planted. We can grow them."

"The first year, we didn't have enough greenhouses

to start what we needed. We purchased starts, but that ate up our profit. Drew suggested these little consumer-grade greenhouses. Parents had donated a few, and we were able to acquire a few more. Drew got them set up and we cut our seedling costs dramatically. Ever since, I've had parents, kids, and teachers scouring the garage sales and end of season sales to find them."

"Who is Drew?" Candace asked.

"Drew is our custodian and superhero. He's basically a full-time gardener who does some handyman stuff."

"He's awesome," said Miriam.

Gene agreed. "One of the board members is on the board of the local conservation district. He asked us if we could grow ferns for some of their projects." He led the group through the sheltered space, pointing out red osier dogwood and Douglas spirea starts, before segueing back to his earlier lecture. "Having growing contracts allows us to have a stable source of income, and we find it easy to divide tasks among the grades based on their learning objectives."

"Why do you have so many different types of growing areas?" Candace asked.

"We start the plants in the greenhouses, then move them to the cold frames. Depending on their destination, some are then planted out in the fields. That's mainly the food crops. The natives usually stay in the cold frames until the year before they are sold. We make sure all the natives are hardy enough to survive a frost before selling them on."

Irene monitored Candace out of the corner of her eye. The other woman looked bedraggled, and Irene remembered she was still pumping breast milk.

"It's an impressive setup," she summed up, taking another glance around. "But my caffeine level is dipping. Do you think we can go back to the office?"

Irene caught a flicker of annoyance on Gene's face, quickly shuttered. Candace looked relieved. Miriam changed direction to go along with the plan, and the group made their way back to the school.

After a break, Irene returned to Gene's office. "Candace needs a few more minutes. She's still breastfeeding her youngest and needs to pump. Let's go over a few of the big questions while we're waiting. I'll catch her up if I need."

Gene and Miriam indicated their agreement.

"As we explained before," Irene started, "we're here because your former business manager, Phyllis Dixon, has made a variety of allegations about the school and its finances."

Miriam snorted in derision.

"One of her biggest concerns, and it's backed up by your own records, is the extensive reimbursements Gene is collecting. It's come up as a finding in the last couple of audits. Can you tell me—us"—Irene amended as Candace entered the office—"why you have purchased so much for reimbursement, rather than using more public contracting methods?"

Gene shrugged. "Time is of the essence."

"I'm sure you're aware that Ms. Dixon's accusations and concerns have raised questions and scrutiny."

"I'm aware," he said.

Irene waited a moment, hoping he would provide additional information. "This isn't the kind of thing that you can stonewall into going away."

"I'm not stonewalling," he replied firmly. "I'm being careful."

"Careful enough that you're not making it easy."

"I love this school. I believe it serves a valuable purpose in the community. I can't let one bad hiring decision risk it."

Sensing Irene was floundering, Candace stepped in. "Our job is to ensure that tax paper money has been used appropriately. We have a credible whistleblower who has pointed out a variety of oversights and discrepancies. As someone who comes from a position of leadership, what do you think should happen at this point?"

Gene's gaze held steady. "I think it should be investigated."

"Should we ask a team from the State Education Commission to perform a program audit?" Candace suggested.

There were a few moments of silence while Gene considered the question. "I didn't realize that was an option."

"Part of investigating a financial claim is ensuring the money was spent in accordance with program goals."

Irene was surprised Candace had played this card, as they had not talked about this possibility. It was a smart decision.

Gene hesitated before replying. "The school will do its best to support any investigations the state deems appropriate. However, our curriculum is a matter between us and the community, not the state."

In Oregon, a charter school could be operated by community members under a contract with the local board of education. The school was a separate legal entity. While a charter school had to follow some of the same laws as district public school, it could ignore others. Charter schools could be set up for a variety of reasons, including language immersion, technical learning, or specialized learning. It was rare for the state to step in asking questions about programs or curriculum.

Candace acknowledged his comment. "Irene and I will focus on the potential misappropriation of funds, in line with Phyllis Dixon's complaint. But it will be important for us to understand the structural use of funds as well. The school does not have an unlimited right to use educational funding."

"I understand," he said.

And silence fell. Again.

Feeling like she was butting up against a brick wall, Irene looked at her notes to find a way forward. "Can you tell us about the incident which led to Ms. Dixon's termination?"

Gene scowled. "I'd rather not comment."

Again, Candace stepped in. "There is already an investigation. It will all come out in the end."

"Yes, but you are not leading the investigation. My lawyer has advised me to only discuss the issue with the actual investigators."

Irene felt a rare surge of frustration. "Alright. Let's talk about the enrollment discrepancies."

Gene's scowl became more intense. He remained silent.

Her gaze moving anxiously between Irene and Gene, Miriam offered, "Maybe we should invite Chick to join us?"

Chapter 4

Charlotte Roy entered the small office like the first daffodil of spring, tentative but welcome. She was a tall, bosomy woman around Irene's age. Her long blond hair was naturally starting to add some gray, and unnatural ribbons of color rioted among the cheerful chaos. A variety of clips held some strands away from her friendly face and laughing brown eyes. She was wearing an orange tee shirt and silver and turquoise squash blossom necklace. Her pants were vertically striped in purple and orange and had a bellbottom shape. Bangles and bracelets were arranged on her wrists, and her fingers sported a variety of rings.

The effect was so familiar, so similar to her friend Sharon, that it took Irene a moment to realize they hadn't met. They weren't friends. That Irene didn't even know her.

Miriam had left the room while they were waiting for Charlotte. She had informed the group that she couldn't add much to the attendance conversation, and Gene had suggested she return to her classroom.

Charlotte crossed the office and reached out to shake hands. Irene responded by rote, then watched Charlotte shake Candace's hand and take a seat. Bemused from the surge of familiarity, Irene took out her notes.

"Ms. Roy—"

"Please, call me 'Chick'. I prefer it."

Irene laughed in surprise. "That must be a story."

Chick's bracelets rattled as she waved that away. "Not really. I loved chickens when I was a kid—I still do—so my big brother started calling me Chick. I loved it then and I love it now, though there were a few years in the middle when the nickname suffered from disuse."

Irene inclined her head in understanding. "Well, thank you for meeting with us. We're here—"

"I know," Chick said dismissively. "Gene told me."

"Okay. Well, then, Gene tells me you use a software program to track registrations and attendance."

Chick named a popular software designed for the purpose. "The teachers can mark attendance on a tablet, and it is immediately viewable to the front office."

"Right. I understand you and Phyllis Dixon had some arguments about access to the computer as well as reporting?"

Chick widened her eyes dramatically. "God, yes. She had access to the software. All the staff do. But she was blocked from seeing personal information about the students. The software only allows staff who are in contact with the child to view information. And then, only some of it. Things like address, social security numbers, medical history, and parental information are available on a need-to-know basis. There was no reason that Phyllis should have needed to know much about the kids. Her job was finance, not working with the kids."

"What information did she want?"

Chick shrugged. "She claimed she wanted to verify attendance numbers but that information was none of her business."

Gene clarified. "Phyllis felt she should be able to ensure no potential revenue sources were being overlooked. I repeatedly denied her access to that information."

"Why?"

Gene paused, formulating his reply. "Many of these families are undocumented. They live in fear of the government. We've spent years convincing them to send their children here. It's important for us to guard student details."

"Okay. You didn't think she needed access, but she clearly disagreed. What did she say were her reasons for wanting access?"

"As I said, she wanted to confirm revenue sources."

"Right. But what did she want to check? The number of students? Daily attendance? What?"

Chick stepped in. "Children go through an enrollment process before they start attending school and renew that each year. That's our base enrollment. From there, we use the program to take attendance, review schedules, and report grades. Among other things. As part of the registration process, parents sign up for an e-alert that sends out weather delays, permission forms, or unexcused absences. One of the things I know Phyllis wanted access to was the absence information. She thought we might be able to apply for additional funding if any analysis showed deviation from standard patterns."

Gene snorted in derision. "That's a generous interpretation."

Chick grimaced. "Well, I do have to admit I doubted her sincerity on that."

Irene looked back and forth between them. "So, what do you think her motivation was?"

Gene explained. "Some of the kids come in without

the best track record. Phyllis was aware of who those children were and where they were assigned."

Chick blew out an exasperated breath. "Now, that's generous. What she wanted"—she confided to Candace who was sitting next to her, but at a volume clear to the rest of the room—"was to keep an eye on them and tattle."

Gene scowled at her repressively. "As business manager, her contact with the children was limited. Over time, I tried to limit it even more. It tended to go badly." He grimaced in memory. "But it was part of her job. She worked with the farming profit centers, which meant interacting with the students."

Chick rolled her eyes. "Just tell them, Gene."

He scowled. "Until the wrongful termination case is over—"

"It'll be easier if you come out with it."

Scowling, Gene gave in. "There were a variety of incidents, but the last one was the killing blow."

Apparently feeling Gene wasn't going quickly enough, Chick took over. "One of the programs had a rather expensive accident. Phyllis became irate and abusive with the project leader, who was a minor. The teacher in charge of the program tried to intervene. She asked Phyllis to calm down and attempted to lead the minor away. Phyllis grabbed the child and continued to berate her. Before the teacher could intervene, the teen became angry and pushed Ms. Dixon, calling her a 'fucking bitch'."

"I'll tell the rest, Chick. Thank you." A look passed between Gene and Chick that Irene read as a warning. "Ms. Dixon wanted to file charges against the minor, but I convinced her not to."

"Not that I think her behavior was acceptable," Candace interjected carefully, "but why didn't you let her? It sounds like Ms. Dixon would have faced charges as well?"

"Having police come to the school isn't good for the students," Gene said carefully.

"Why not?"

Gene continued speaking carefully and precisely. "When the police come, some of the students panic. Some even leave the school grounds."

"You mean they go home?" Candace asked. "Their parents come and get them?"

"No. The kids head out cross-country to where their parents are working."

Candace looked startled. "That sounds dangerous."

"It is," Chick confirmed. "They cross highways and travel miles in order to get home. Last year we had a hit-and-run incident with one of the kids riding a bicycle. Thankfully, he wasn't hurt, but anything could have happened."

Irene thought of her nephews. "Aren't you concerned that something else will happen?"

Gene gestured in agreement. "Of course. And, of course, it did. The next day, Phyllis waited in the parking lot for the child to be dropped off by her parents. She handed the parents a bill for the equipment that had been damaged and warned them that unless they paid it, she would pursue the matter of assault. I tried to prevent the interaction, but she was too quick."

"How did the parents react?"

"Badly. I'd rather not go into that part."

"Is the child okay?" Candace asked.

"We're still rebuilding trust," Gene admitted. "But

she's physically okay and still attending the school."

Irene thought about this story for a bit. "And this incident led to Phyllis' termination?"

"Yes." Flat and barren as a salt flat.

Irene and Candace exchanged a glance. Candace subtly waved a finger in a way that suggested they should move on.

"Going back to the attendance information," Irene redirected. "What is the discrepancy that the education district is concerned about?"

Chick frowned. "We turn in a monthly attendance report. It captures overall enrollment but also shows average attendance and special services usage."

"Remind us what special services are?" Irene requested.

"Students who need special services. English as a second language or learning disabilities. Anyway, the discrepancy between the reports is in those numbers."

"What was the difference?" Irene asked.

Gene stepped in. "The reports the district received reported higher special services numbers than we wanted to report. We can back up those numbers with actual students, but Chick and I usually underreport special services."

Irene was taken aback. "Why would you do that?"

Gene tapped his fingers restlessly. "While we do get additional money for students enrolled in special services, in some cases I feel we don't need to report that information. For example, we try to mainstream the ESL students. More than half the teachers speak Spanish, and many parents see participating in a partially Spanish classroom as a bonus. We make it work, and I don't want to report for the additional money."

"There is some discretion in filling out the reports, and we have a system," Chick jumped in. "The district received reports that were signed by Gene and me, but the numbers had been adjusted."

"How do you think that happened?" Irene asked.

"I don't know," Chick admitted. "The signatures were digital, which should have locked the document."

"I don't know, either," Gene said. "But I have my suspicions. Phyllis was unusually interested in those reports."

Irene's eyes narrowed. "Did she have anything to do with their preparation?"

"No. But she used them in her monthly billing to the district as backup. A few months before she was dismissed, we had several discussions about how our underreporting was costing us money."

Chick made a noise and rolled her eyes again. "Discussions? Full on shouting matches."

"Thank you, Chick." Gene tried to tamp down Chick's commentary.

"In other words," Irene said, "you were underreporting special services even though you could have received additional funding? And then, the reports were modified to show special services in line with actuals?"

The school staffers gestured their agreement.

"And you both have suspicions that Ms. Dixon had something to with it, but you haven't followed up?"

Gene shrugged. "We have fixed whatever was going on. Pursuing the topic means more contact with her. That isn't in the school's best interest." He paused, then said. "I know what these kids need."

Irene saw what she had been searching for. Gene

cared about these kids so much he might go too far to protect them. With his control and intelligence, Irene thought it would be difficult to assess where too far was.

She looked at Candace, giving her the floor. Candace shook her head.

"I think that's all the questions we have for Chick," Irene summarized. "I do have an additional question for Gene, so you can take off if you need to, Chick."

Smiling, Chick rose and shook Irene's and Candace's hands before she left. "Nice to meet you. Let me know if you need anything."

Irene turned back to Gene. "Do you had any questions for us?"

Gene studied his hands thoughtfully. "Where do we go from here?"

Irene looked to Candace. Technically, Candace was the lead investigator, though she had let Irene ask the majority of questions. Candace reviewed her notes. "We need to come back and interview key staff members." She pointed to a list in her papers. "I'd like to explore the reimbursements more thoroughly. I'm going to check with the state education department about possible program issues—"

Gene cut her off. "Program issues?"

Candace gestured at her notes. "State money needs to be spent in a certain way. I want to assure myself that none of the agricultural programs are in conflict with state education criteria."

Gene didn't respond, but his nostrils flared with anger.

"I'd also like to resolve the enrollment reporting. I understand what you're saying, but it's one of the easiest things to get wrong. It's a simple matter to falsify student enrollment in order to obtain additional funding or claim to provide services they are not offering."

"But we've sorted all that out with the district," Gene pointed out. "The extra money was returned."

"I understand," Candace agreed. "But it needs to be reviewed. It's also an obvious weakness that should be corrected."

Irene added, "I'd like to review the for-profit companies the school is running."

"They are barely making any money," Gene protested.

"We want to check the legitimacy of expenses to ensure the funds and expenses are recorded appropriately."

Gene had been growing more agitated as they talked. "We aren't doing anything wrong."

"I know it's hard," Candace soothed, "especially when you haven't been breaking the rules. But we have to investigate Ms. Dixon's claims before we can dismiss them."

Gene tried to regain control. "I understand."

Sympathetically, Irene offered, "This is hard, but try to think of it as any other audit. Audits always find something, but that provides an opportunity to improve."

Gene shot her a skeptical look.

Irene shrugged. "Okay, you're right. Try not to focus on it. Let the chips fall where they may."

Candace asked, "One thing I was curious about…" She trailed off.

"Yes?" Gene prompted.

"Well, it doesn't have to do with the audit, but I was curious about burnout. While we were on the tour, you were doing lots of little jobs. The programs rely on after school support and community involvement. Does that equal a high overtime burden?"

Gene shrugged dismissively. Then, after a moment, said, "It can be an issue. We do our best to pay for each teacher's time so they aren't working for free. But I also think most of the teachers and staff love the program."

"Why?" Irene asked bluntly.

Gene paused to consider the question. "I got into teaching to help kids, not administer tests. Flexible programs help all students succeed."

"That's impressive, but surely there must be failures? Problems? Stressors?" Irene pushed.

Gene looked out the window, studying the fields. Irene sensed he wasn't stalling so much as finding the right words. "I can't speak for how the entire staff feels. The sacrifices are worth it for me. Some teachers do move on. The first few years had high staff turnover. Even now, the staff differs about some of the program. But I see something here that I didn't see in conventional schools. The kids are able to take what we are trying to teach them and put it into a real-life environment. I hear the kids say, 'I don't want to be a farmer.' But I see those same kids start to take math and science more seriously, and work to hit their goals so they can work on the business side instead in horticulture."

To make sure his point was understood, Gene met Irene's eyes directly. "And the kids who like the hands on? They start finding a way to succeed. They want to earn the right to participate in the programs." He paused, then admitted, "Not all the kids respond. No matter what you do, you can't reach some of them."

"If a particular subject or program is not their thing, we encourage them to find something that is," Gene admitted. "I don't want this to be a prison camp. I want this to be a place where learning starts to make sense. If they want to move to another school, we do our best."

He rubbed the side of his face wearily. "Maintenance is always on my mind. I'd love to be able to hire more maintenance workers." After a few beats, he continued, "And there's always a list of things that I wish we do better or have someone specialize in. But I think everyone who stays loves the program."

Chapter 5

In her email that evening, Irene found an email from Marion County Dog Control.

*Hello Irene,*

*Thanks for bringing in that dog the other day. We're calling him Max. He's quite the character.*

*His three-day hold will be up tomorrow, and he's showing some signs of kennel stress. According to the notes, you said you might be willing to take him as a foster. I think he'd do better in a home than here.*

*Let us know if you want to give him a try.*

*Ashley*

Irene studied the message. Then she pondered Percy's picture with the large rosette from his Agility Dog Champion run. Irene thought about Gene's Schuster's resolution to save the children in his care.

She typed back. *Okay. I can pick him up Saturday morning. What time?*

\*\*\*\*

Irene arrived at the shelter moments after it opened Saturday. It was already busy. A young couple was at the desk, filling out paperwork and listening to a shelter worker talk about reclaiming their dog. A mother with two boys looked through a three-ring binder of potential dogs. Staff technicians moved about the facility. A pair of men with INMATE marked on their orange shirts pushed mops in the farthest corridors.

After Irene approached the desk and explained why she was there, the staffer picked up the phone. "Ashley, Max's foster is here." She listened for a moment and then put down the phone. "She'll be out in a moment."

Irene took a seat until Ashley popped out behind a security door. "Hi, Irene. Let's go back here and talk for a minute." She gestured to a class office to the side. "This is your first foster. Do you have any questions?"

"I don't think so. I simply take him and work with him until he's adopted?"

"Basically. Get to know him. Tell us about him. Find out if he's housetrained, how he acts around things. If there are any behavior issues, we need to let potential adopters about them. He still needs to be neutered and get the rest of his shots. You can take him to those."

"When is his appointment?"

"His appointment is for"—Ashley checked her notes—"February twenty-seventh. A couple of weeks. They'll do the second set of shots then too. If you end up keeping him over a month, you'll need to bring him in for flea treatments and a couple other shots."

"Wow, the neuter is two weeks out. That's quite a while."

"We contract with Oregon Humane Society, and they have a low-cost spay and neuter program. They work us in quickly."

"So, I'll have him at least a couple of weeks."

"Yes. He can't get adopted until he's neutered. But he can do meet and greets. If someone falls for him, they can put a hold on him. Anything you can tell us about him is great. He's been really sweet, but definitely energetic. If he gets to be more than you can handle, let us know. We can help problem solve. Don't take him to a dog park. We don't want him attacking or getting attacked by anyone."

Irene agreed.

"There is an emergency protocol in this folder." She showed Irene a folder, then tucked it into a bag filled with food, piddle pads, toys, and bowls. "So, are you ready?"

"Release the hound," Irene said with a smile.

Moments later, Max exploded from the back room and across the linoleum floor. The shelter had bathed him, and his medium-length gray-and-black fur glistened. In a flurry of excitement, he careened toward anyone who might pay attention to him. A waiting family took a step back. The mopping inmates looked wary.

Irene crouched down and clicked her tongue to get his attention. With an ecstatic look on his face, he charged toward her. He launched himself at her. Irene overbalanced and toppled onto her butt. While the dog draped across her chest, nuzzling and licking her face, Irene concentrated on preventing a French kiss.

The dog was on a six-foot leash, but Ashley was still having trouble reeling him in enough to get him off Irene. While not a big dog, his power and excitement were awesome. Ashley got his attention with a cookie. He stood beside her, quivering with anticipation. She lured him into a sit.

"As you can see, he has a ways to go."

Irene stood up. Ashley handed his leash to her. Irene used a treat she had stuffed in her pocket to capture his attention.

"Here's the bag," Ashley said, loading the bag into Irene's other hand.

"Okay, thanks." Irene turned to go. "Oh, yeah." She

turned around again. "Is Max his name? Or did you give him a name?"

"We just named him. He's a stray. We couldn't find an owner."

"Could I pick a new name?"

"Sure. Let us know." Ashley smiled and turned back down the hall.

****

The dog sat alertly in his crate, enjoying the view. Irene drove the few miles to home, parked, and opened the car door. Before letting him out, she checked what kind of collar the shelter had given him. Because he was so quick and agile, she wanted to make sure it was a something that would tighten if he tried to slip it. The collar was the type known as a fitted martingale so Irene felt assured he couldn't get loose if he bolted. Taking a firm grip on the leash, she opened the kennel door. For the first time, he didn't explode from the kennel. He popped his head out, looked around, and then stood there looking at her.

"Come on, buddy," Irene encouraged.

He looked down at the ground and back at her. *Surely you are kidding. I could hurt myself.*

"Dude, you did it before. I remember."

He jumped down and trotted to the nearest bush.

Irene walked him around the block, with the dog pulling and jerking as much as expected. The leash didn't bother him, and he gamely smelled all the smells.

Irene believed that dogs who are walked regularly feel more secure. They can check their pee-mail, sniff out what's going on, and then come home. Therefore, her plan was to take Max on hourly walks around the neighborhood.

They got back to the house, and she showed him the car and kennel again before heading inside. Irene noticed he paused at the steps and then at the doorway, but once inside, he looked around with interest.

Keeping her hold on the leash, Irene took him to the kitchen and showed him the water dish. He took a big slurp. She gave him a cookie, and then walked him around the house, still on leash. He sniffed diligently. A couple of times he came to a corner and took a couple of prancing steps, as though he wanted to lift his leg, but a touch on the leash and a "No" stopped him.

After this successful tour, Irene took him on another walk, this time around the opposite block. Upon returning to the house, Irene introduced him to the fenced back yard. She dropped the leash and let him drag it. She walked the perimeter of the fence, taking the opportunity to look for any areas needing repair and also luring the dog to explore. Her house was in downtown Salem, so the yard wasn't large. The dog absorbed it all.

Irene sat outside on the back steps and watched the dog explore. She praised him whenever he lifted his leg outside. After about ten minutes, she picked up his leash and headed inside. Another tour of the small house before she put him in Percy's old kennel with its old dog bed. She had washed the entire setup, but the dog sniffed all the surfaces. Irene was sure he could smell the old dog.

The dog sat in the kennel, looking around and sniffing. She read for fifteen minutes, then she took him for another walk. They repeated the walk-then-relax pattern twice more, then she prepared her lunch. He watched her with a hungry eye. By evening, they had taken a dozen short walks, racking up over sixteen thousand steps on her Fitbit. The dog looked more relaxed and already walked better on leash, having grasped the idea that they were to move forward on the little concrete paths.

At dinner, Irene offered him kibble, and he scarfed it up, licking his chops and eyeing her suspiciously. Irene noted the signs of resource guarding. Most dogs, rescue or not, understood the concept of "mine"—my food, my ball, my favorite spot. There was a natural tendency to protect what was "mine." Well-socialized dogs were taught that everything is the human's, who grant the dog high-value items. When dogs did not understand the concept, they snapped, growled, or generally behaved in ways humans don't appreciate. Irene added the issue to her list and made a note to work on it tomorrow.

He supervised her dinner preparation intently, showing an increasingly keen interest in food. They watched TV or read for the rest of the evening, then after letting him outside one last time, Irene settled him into a second kennel in her bedroom. He slept through the night.

****

The next morning, Irene got up and made sure to hurry him outside. He did his thing and then ate breakfast with gusto. She took him for a long walk, expanding the territory from yesterday's repetitive circuit. He walked forward at a brisk pace at the end of his leash, sniffing and darting for interesting scents.

The dog seemed so content, Irene decided to go to church. She reasoned this would allow her to gauge his reaction to being alone before she had to work the next day. Giving him a toy stuffed with frozen treats, Irene headed to church.

Irene arrived mere moments before service started. She said hello to her mother, Jennifer, as she slid into the pew next to her. The service went smoothly, and the preacher was refreshingly pithy.

When service had ended, Irene got up, intending to leave quickly. "Bye, Jennifer. I have to run."

"Irene, I need to talk to you," Jennifer commanded.

Irene closed her eyes, cursing silently. She turned back to face Jennifer. "What's up?"

"I have an idea, but I need you to help."

"I need to get home," Irene said impatiently. "Can this wait?"

"Why are you in such a hurry?" Jennifer complained.

Irene braced herself. "I have a foster dog—"

"Oh, not another dog. You finally got rid of the last one."

Irene's jaw clenched. She counted to five. "Yes. I am fostering a dog."

"I thought you were done with that dog stuff."

"Percy died. I never said I was done with *dog stuff*."

"But with your MS, do you think—"

Irene cut her off. "Jennifer. I need to get back. What did you want?"

Jennifer pursed her lips. "Well, I wanted to get your help with a charity event."

"No."

She looked hurt. "I haven't even told you what it's for."

"It doesn't matter. I have a full-time job. I don't have time."

"*I* have a full-time job, and *I* have time."

Irene wondered if it was worth trying to explain to

her that being a realtor, with its flexible hours and emphasis on networking, had a different set of challenges than working as a forensic accounting investigator for the state. Carefully, she said, "Regardless, I don't want to work on a charity event."

"It's for you. My idea is a Margaritas for MS night."

Irene wanted to weep. "Jennifer. *Please* listen to me. I don't want to be part of this."

"Why not? You have MS."

"Yes, I do. It's difficult. I don't want to talk about it. Most people with MS try not to drink alcohol."

"I know. I thought we could also offer virgin margaritas. I thought you'd be pleased I was taking an interest. And it was be a great way for us both to meet people. I mean, you might meet some nice young doctor who would—"

"I'm going to stop you there. My answer is no."

"Why are you being so stubborn?" Jennifer accused.

"I have no idea where I could have got it from."

"Fine. But I haven't given up. I'll find something we can do together."

Irene looked at her. "When did that become a goal?"

"Well, remember a few months back, when you said we had a hard time connecting because we don't have similar interests? I'm trying to find something we both like."

"I meant something like bird watching or Bible study, not creating a big project that we'd slave to put together." Irene looked at her watch. "Let's talk about his later. I didn't want to leave this dog on his own for more than a couple of hours." She leaned over to give Jennifer a light hug. "See you later."

Jennifer gave her a squeeze back. "Yes."

Irene found the dog lying in his kennel, chewing on the chew toy with enjoyment. He greeted her enthusiastically then followed her outside for a break. He stretched into a play bow. *What did you think I'd do?*

She stroked his ears for a moment, then put him on leash for a quick tour around the block.

Chapter 6

Irene walked into the office Monday, tired from the long weekend of walks, but happy with the dog's progress. She was struck by the tension filling the room. People seemed to be working in an unnaturally focused way. She spotted Peter angrily reorganizing the folders on his desk. Nearby, Candace typed as though the keyboard had offended her.

Irene put down her bags and flipped on her computer. She scanned the inbox. Unenlightened, her attention swung back to Peter's desk. The office became unnaturally quiet.

"Here you go, Peter," Candace enunciated, flopping a stack of paper onto his desk. "They all have folders."

Peter tossed his head dramatically and looked at the file numbers. "Thank you, Candace. This makes it easy to see that these files are not mine."

As if following a tennis match, Irene shifted to Candace.

"I'm in over my head. I don't have time to finish these reports."

"I understand your dilemma, but that doesn't mean I have to finish them."

"John told me that he was going to ask you to take over these."

"He hasn't said anything about that to me."

Candace set her jaw. "I understand *your* dilemma,

but they are yours now."

"I'll check with John and let you know," he said.

"Fine." Candace turned to walk off.

"But in the meantime—" Peter lifted the stack of files from his desk as though they were toxic waste. "—these do not belong in my desk. They need to filed."

Candace snatched the files from him and stalked toward the break room, heaving the papers into a basket marked "To Be Filed" as she passed by.

Slowly, the office went back to work.

Peter met Irene's eyes defiantly, then returned to his computer.

Irene wanted some coffee, but knew if she stepped into the break room, Candace would want to rehash the argument with her. The entire office could hear her whispering violently with some other staffer.

Candace and Peter had a long-running disagreement over all things file-related. Over the years, Irene had heard every possible variation of the story. Candace didn't file correctly. Peter didn't make allowances. Both were true, but ridiculous.

Irene thought the personality clash between Candace and Peter needed to be addressed, but John brushed her concerns aside. He claimed each party was an adult and the argument only harmed themselves. Irene saw each time they engaged in their battle, weeks of snide remarks and stiff silence clouded the office, drenching the occupants in negativity.

She elected to forgo coffee until the coast was clear.

Twenty minutes later, she was finishing an email regarding her investigation of a sheriff's office when Candace approached her cubicle. "Irene, can I talk to you?"

Irene looked up from her screen. "Sure. Give me five minutes and I'll meet you in the small conference room." Irene finished the email, hit send, grabbed a cup of coffee, and was down the hall well before the five minutes were up.

Candace was waiting, still steaming. "I know you are friends with Peter, but he can be really annoying," Candace told her, apparently believing Irene had the power to adjudicate the matter.

Irene settled into a conference chair and took a sip of coffee before responding. "Most humans tend to be annoying."

Catching the warning in Irene's tone, Candace snapped, "He makes a big deal about the office protocols. Even if the files weren't transferred to him, he could have passed them on."

"So could you."

"But I'm too busy," Candace wailed. "I can't get through my workload. That's why John told me to give some of my cases to Peter. Peter is well suited to deal with finishing those cases."

Irene studied her. "What I hear you saying is that you're falling behind and hoped Peter could help you. Did you ask him for help?"

Candace looked away. "No. John said I could give him the cases."

Irene wanted to offer sympathy but could only offer a small smile. "Peter can be fussy, but he has a good heart. He shouldn't have been so hard on you, but if you ask him, I bet he'll help."

Candace's expression turned sulky. "I shouldn't have to explain to an underling."

Irene's eyebrows shot up. "Underling?" It wasn't

the first time Irene had noticed Candace's sensitivity to the office pecking order. She and Candace were senior investigators, while Peter was a junior investigator. That was one rung on a slippery ladder.

"Oh, you know what I mean."

Irene didn't, but let it go. "Did you only want to talk about Peter?"

Candace shook her head. "I wanted to find out what you were thinking about the Fallbrook case."

Irene thought about it. "I think there is cause for concern. The reimbursement situation has been brought up each year during the annual audit. School equipment flows around the community, though I'll be surprised if it leads to anything." She paused, frowning. "The enrollment discrepancy seems… off, somehow."

"What do you mean?"

Irene formed her words carefully. "The county education district shows one set of enrollment data. The files at the school match that data. But the registrar's program reports a different set. Chick swears up and down she uses the program to fill out the report."

Candace looked through a stack of papers in front of her. "Yes. The county reports show more ESL students than the registrar's program does. Phantom students. It's a common form of fraud."

"When I spoke to Gene, he told me they traditionally underreported the ESL students. A few years ago, they did an analysis and found that applying for grants was more lucrative than the extra money from the county. He and the board don't want to be accused of double-dipping."

Now Candace scowled. "Don't we have some guidance on that?"

Irene offered the rule. "County enrollment can be augmented with outside funds."

"So why underreport?"

Irene shrugged. "I think the real mystery is how the reports got changed and why. If the form was approved by Gene and filed on the server, how was a different report inserted in its place?"

"Do you think an education department audit might point us in the right direction?"

"What do you think that would reveal?"

"I'm not sure. Giving the children money for the year-end trip could be problematic."

Irene thought for a moment.

As a forensic accountant, her job focused on embezzled money and fraud. She set out to prove funds had been stolen or misused and to demonstrate how it had occurred. As with many jobs, people often asked her to address difficulties outside the scope of these endeavors. Irene frequently had to explain she did not perform bookkeeping or general audits.

In her position with the state of Oregon, she frequently found herself called on when someone didn't like a financial situation, regardless of whether or not a forensic audit was needed. It was difficult to explain that a crime had not been committed simply because someone put money into the wrong place.

The issues at Fallbrook were human resources, enrollment, and accounting. The only one she could address was the accounting. The accounting problem stemmed from the large reimbursements going to a particular individual outside a public procurement process. The annual audits had caught the issue, and it had been reported as part of those reports. The school's board knew and understood the situation. And had chosen not to take action.

"It's your case, so I'll do whatever you decide. But if it was my case, I'd review the enrollment data, scan through the reimbursements, and mark it finished. There is nothing we need to prosecute."

Candace thought about her words for a moment. "Let's do some more interviews and talk to the education department. I understand your point, but if the county is nervous, I think we need to investigate this thoroughly."

Irene dug for patience. Candace wanted to slow things down; Irene wanted to resolve the problem quickly. "Sure. But unless something else comes up, it doesn't sound like there is a case to prosecute."

Candace, who had a rep for needing to know every detail, no matter how small or insignificant, responded sharply. "Are we here to find out the truth? Or just to get rid of the problem as quickly as possible?"

"It's your case, Candace. I'll do what you ask."

"Do you know anyone over in the education department?" Candace asked.

Irene shook her head.

"Alright. I'll find someone to talk to."

Irene mentally reviewed her notes. "The board okayed those trips, but I'd still like to find out the source of funding."

"That's a good point." Another moment passed. "Phyllis Dixon says Gene is somehow profiting from all this. I wonder if we should explore why she believes that?"

"When we interview her, we'll bring that up."

****

After talking to Candace, Irene returned to her desk.

"Peter, I'm going to go get a coffee. Want to join me?" Going to get coffee was code for wanting to discuss something in private.

Peter jumped up. "Sure."

"Okay, spill it," Irene said as soon as they were out the door, walking to the coffee stand in the next building.

Obviously still upset by the insult, Peter growled. "She dumped a huge stack of paper on my desk and walked off."

Irene glanced over at him. "Seriously?" Peter had a flare for drama and could make a mountain out of a molehill. Given enough time, he usually came back to a more realistic assessment. Clearly enough time had not passed.

Peter elaborated. "Friday afternoon, I found a stack of paper in my inbox. No note, not sorted, nothing. I asked around and found it was from her. I asked her about it. She said John told her to give it to me. I was upset, but I tracked down the file and tidied it up. Followed up on a couple small things."

"That was kind. Thank you."

"When I left for lunch, I came back and found another stack," he said. "I was due in a meeting, so I couldn't ask her about it right away. When I got done with the meeting, she had dumped another stack in my inbox. I asked her about it, and she claimed to be doing some spring cleaning and John had told her to shift these files to me."

Peter paused to open a door, letting Irene enter first. The warm, cozy smell brushed against their faces. As they took their place in line, he continued, "I pointed out that it was common courtesy to pass paperwork with the accompanying folder. She said she didn't have time to fool with paperwork."

The barista took their order, and they moved to end of the counter. "And?" Irene prompted.

Peter looked embarrassed. "I waited for her to leave for the day, then dumped the papers back in her in box, attaching the filing procedure."

"Seriously?" Irene studied him. "You are going to war over filing?"

"Yes. She needs to do her J.O.B."

Irene found it hard to argue.

After the barista slid Irene's drink across the counter, she took a sip.

"I'm sick of her dumping her work on us," Peter said passionately. "She spends all her time texting her family, then asks us to clean up what she doesn't get done."

The barista slid Peter's drink across the counter but he ignored it.

Irene gestured to the drink. "Fix up your drink, then let's sit out on the benches."

A few minutes passed before they were ensconced on the bench, out of easy hearing distance. "She's not going to change, Peter."

"It's not fair," he muttered, taking a sip of his drink.

"You're right. She isn't following procedure with the files. But it is a small world. Even if one of you eventually leave the department, you'll meet again. She may be on a committee or hiring panel. Is this battle worth the war?"

"Why doesn't John do something?" Peter ground out.

Irene shrugged. "She's a qualified and competent investigator. She's meticulous, which means slow. She's friendly and John likes her. She goes out of her way to stay on his good side."

"It's not fair," Peter repeated.

Irene kept her face sympathetic. "Do what you want, but my advice is to reach out and offer some help. Be the bigger person, but don't make a big deal about it."

Chapter 7

Irene's mornings had fallen into an unusually fraught rhythm. She arrived at the office on Wednesday morning, prepared for an interview with Phyllis Dixon. She and Candace had strategized the appointment to elicit key pieces of information they needed.

But Candace wasn't there. She had called and left messages with John, Irene, and the receptionist, Mishel, that she and her family had come down with the flu. Irene felt a sense of dread. She had been counting on Candace to help her out. While she always tried to remain neutral, Irene was prepared to dislike Phyllis Dixon.

Mishel buzzed to announce her visitor had arrived. Irene checked the small meeting room, then walked to the lobby.

Phyllis Dixon was in her late fifties and was dressed formally. Her hair was striking white platinum, cut into a severe bob that framed her large features well. She wore tasteful jewelry, and a dark green, elegant shirtfront dress paired with a hand-knit scarf. Her make-up was noticeable, but well applied. She could have been going to a job interview.

Irene approached her and held out her hand. "Ms. Dixon, I'm Irene Lisner."

Phyllis took her hand and returned her handshake. "Nice to meet you."

"Let's go to a conference room," Irene said, opening

the door and gesturing Phyllis inside. "Can I offer you some coffee or water?"

"No, thank you," Phyllis said.

Once settled into a small conference room, Irene gestured to her own coffee, which she had placed in the room before greeting Phyllis. "I hope you don't mind if I drink my coffee."

"No. I had coffee with my breakfast," Phyllis stated with precision.

"I'm addicted," Irene admitted. "I keep waiting for someone to ask me if I have a hobby. I'm going to answer, 'drinking coffee.'"

Phyllis didn't smile.

"Thank you for meeting with me," Irene offered.

Phyllis nodded.

"We have some questions we'd like you to help us with," Irene explained.

Phyllis nodded again.

Irene reminded herself not to roll her eyes. "The case has been in the department for a few weeks, but I only got the case last week. I've interviewed Gene—"

Phyllis sniffed.

Irene continued, "—Miriam—"

Another sniff.

"—and Chick."

A snort.

Irene picked up a pen. "They took us on a tour of the school and grounds. I should be able to keep up with anything you want to tell me."

Phyllis studied her. "You aren't going to ask me questions?"

"I like to let people tell their own story."

Phyllis sniffed. "I don't think this is a proper way to

testify. There is no one here to record anything. And don't know what you want me to say."

Irene calmed herself before replying, "You aren't testifying today. I'd like to hear what you have to say. We can use it to help guide our investigation."

Phyllis remained silent.

"Let's start with what your duties were at the school," Irene said.

"I was the business manager," Phyllis said, as though explaining to a rather dull child.

"What did that entail?"

"Lots of things."

"Take me through an average day."

"Well, in the morning, there would be various issues about accounting for any money coming in. Kids pay off fines or parents bring in fees. About ten a.m. things settle down, and I'd begin work on billings and payments."

"Did you have any help with that?" Irene asked, making notes.

"No."

"Did you worry about segregation of duties?"

"It's a small office, but we had some basic separation of duty procedures in place. The front desk would collect and open the mail, for example, and stamp any checks. I took care of most of the bookkeeping. Gene would sign all outgoing checks under five thousand dollars, and two board members would have to sign for anything over that or reimbursements for him."

"Did you work in the office for the entire rest of the day?"

"No," Phyllis admitted. "I would move around the campus. I would supervise repairmen or vendors. There were meetings. I left each day for my lunch break."

"Sounds busy," Irene forced appreciation into her voice.

Glad to see Irene understood the difficulty of her job, Phyllis inclined her chin.

After waiting for Phyllis to continue, Irene prompted, "You said you moved around. Where did you go?"

"I met with teachers and other staff."

She resigned herself to dragging Phyllis through the interview. "What did you meet about?"

"I would try to explain the different grant requirements and office protocols." She stopped, appearing to struggle with herself for a moment, but couldn't hold back her words. "But they didn't care. Everyone did what they wanted."

"What do you mean?"

Warming up, Phyllis leaned toward Irene. "We had a grant to help children who had been victims of domestic violence or had been separated from part of their family. The idea was that we'd hire a counselor and set up a fund to help with any costs that might help a child get settled."

"What happened?"

"Well, we got the grant, but then Gene told me that we weren't going to hire another counselor." She paused, waiting for Irene to be as appalled as she was.

Irene searched for the appropriate reaction. "So, you were concerned about supplanting?"

Phyllis looked confused.

"Supplanting. The rule that says you can't replace local funds with federal money. The idea is to prevent writing grants for programs that are already on the ground."

Phyllis looked bemused. "I hadn't heard about that rule. No, I was simply concerned he wasn't using the money appropriately."

Irene made a note. "Are you saying the money didn't go toward victims of domestic violence?"

Phyllis shook her head. "No, it did. Schuster had me put it in a fund and charge some of our counselor's hours to that. And there were other costs."

"So, in the end, he did use the funds in accordance with the grant."

"Yes," Phyllis admitted, disappointed with Irene's calm demeanor. "And then he built that program for," she searched for a word and settled on, "Latinos. He had a program that focused on Spanish-speakers and selling to Mexicans at the farmer's market."

Irene eyed her. "That sounds interesting."

"The program wouldn't accept anyone except these Latino kids." Phyllis stopped, waiting for Irene's response.

Irene waited.

"They were all…illegal aliens," Phyllis muttered. "That's what he cared about. He told me we have an obligation to the students, regardless of their immigration status."

Irene did not immediately respond. She didn't begrudge anyone the occasional inappropriate comment. But Phyllis's tone and body language showed a barely contained rage; her jaw had become more prominent and rigid, her body stiff.

Her response was a cold warning. "The courts have ruled repeatedly that Gene is correct."

Phyllis scoffed. "Oh, please. We shouldn't be wasting money on those kinds of kids."

Thoroughly disgusted, Irene dug for control. "Is there anything else I should know?

"Do you know about the plans for a new school?"

"New school?"

Phyllis huffed. "Yeap. He wants to build a new school. That's why he doesn't want to do any maintenance on this building."

Irene paused to think back. "He told me that they had deferred some costs so they could expand the greenhouse programs."

Smug now, Phyllis corrected Irene. "Last summer he went to the board and convinced them that maintaining the old building wasn't cost-effective. They couldn't get parts for some of the old equipment, and heating costs were huge."

Irene could imagine such a conversation but didn't think it proved Phyllis's point. "And they decided to build a new school?"

"The formed a Building Committee and said they would look into it. But Gene was going to make sure they built him a new school. He's already started buying supplies. Nail guns and lots of other tools."

Irene made some more notes. "Is there an approval process for the tools?"

"Gene doesn't have to get approval for things under five hundred dollars."

"Did he provide receipts? Were they things the school needed?"

"He always provided receipts," Phyllis said grudgingly. "But I don't think we needed any of that stuff. And people take things off the campus. In and out, all the time."

"What do you mean?"

"Gene lets the kids check out equipment. Digital cameras, computers, monitors. And he lets the parents borrow the tables and chairs for events. The auto shop is constantly open. Kids who left the school years ago come around and hang out there. He was always letting some group use the grounds. I told him we needed to at least get waivers, but he said a school should be a hub of the community."

Irene paused from writing notes. "That does sound chaotic. Gene told me he was trying to make the school a community hub."

Phyllis sniffed. "Maybe. But he was giving those kids cash."

"Back up a minute. He was giving what kids cash?"

"All of them. For that after school program. Fizz or whatever they called it."

Irene checked her notes. "FYS? Find Your Success?"

Phyllis nodded. "I told him he needed to track hours and get receipts for things. That if someone got hurt, we'd be in trouble. He always said the board had approved the program and ignored me."

Confused, Irene asked, "Why was he giving them cash?"

Phyllis eyed her scornfully. "He decided to do a 'student work program'. Any of the kids who wanted to work in the program could get extra credit for the hours they worked in the garden program. Any kids who had already graduated but still wanted to work would get minimum wage. He'd always do it in cash. I told him that this would lead to trouble."

"Why did he pay them in cash?"

Phyllis made a disgusted face. "He said some of

them were…" She paused, searching her memory. "Unbanked. You know, they didn't use a bank and so had no way to cash checks without enormous fees."

Irene clarified. "But the school was doing tax withholding for them?"

Phyllis wagged a finger. "Yes, but I told him there would be trouble. And sure enough, a couple of years ago, two of the kids got in a fight. There were knives, and the police got called in. Schuster hushed it all up and closed down the program."

"Was it gang related?"

"I don't know. Someone is always having trouble with someone else."

Irene signaled her understanding. "I understand your concern. What you are describing is unconventional. Did you have procedures in place to try to keep track of all this?"

Phyllis examined her hands. "I followed the rules. I made him give me receipts. I made him get board approval for items over the limits. But I couldn't stop him from bending the rules. I couldn't stop him from making bad policy decisions. He'd tell me, 'Phyllis, when it comes to these kids, I know what's right.'"

"I'm sure you know your concerns are serious," Irene began.

"Of course. I wouldn't have made them otherwise."

"Why did you wait to make them until you were terminated?"

Phyllis's mouth tightened. "I was terminated because I was going to report him."

"What were you going to report?"

Phyllis shifted her gaze away from Irene. "I was going to turn over my information about the school harboring illegal aliens. And there were lots of other things."

Irene was not an expert on immigration law, but she knew the courts ruled repeatedly that schools have an obligation to educate students, regardless of their immigration status. The other items—paying workers in cash, large amounts of reimbursements, allowing school property off the campus—were worth a follow up, but she also knew they had been addressed in the annual audits.

"Let's talk about that. Chick told me you were interested in the registration and attendance information, in spite of Gene telling you it wasn't part of your job duties."

Phyllis snorted. "They didn't want me to see what they were up to."

"Hmmm. Have you heard about the discrepancy between the attendance software and the reports that were turned into the count?"

Phyllis kept her eyes on Irene's face. "No."

Irene waited for a question, but Phyllis did not appear to want more information. Odd. "Thank you for your information, Ms. Dixon. We're aware of your concerns from previous audits. We'll be investigating."

"When will I get to testify?"

"We're a long way from that."

"I want to tell my story," Phyllis insisted.

"We'll let you know if you need to testify," Irene assured her.

"You mean I might not?"

"I don't know. These things take time."

Phyllis sniffed.

Rising from her seat, Irene gestured Phyllis to the

door. "We'll let you know about next steps as soon as possible."

****

It was a disturbing tale, Irene thought returning to her office. She had liked Gene Schuster and did not like Phyllis Dixon. She could see how their personalities would clash.

She grabbed another cup of coffee and was on the way to her desk when John called out to her from his office. "Irene?"

She walked into his office doorway. He gestured for her to have a seat. "Shut the door. How'd this morning go with Phyllis Dixon?"

John Fisher was a trim, confident man whose opinion Irene had learned to value. She shrugged. "Okay. I think she's genuinely concerned but has an axe to grind."

"Fair enough." He rocked back in his chair. "I'm assuming you've heard that Candace is out with the flu."

"Yes. She left me a message because we were supposed to interview Phyllis together."

John tipped his head. "How's it going with her?"

Uncomfortable with the question, Irene took a moment to put together a response. "She's a solid accountant. She has training and is great with details. She knows what has to be done.

John grunted. "Has she told you why she didn't start the case earlier?"

Irene shook her head. She didn't want to be the office snitch.

John grunted again. "Having two senior investigators on this is overkill. We need three working independent investigators. But we need to get this finished."

Irene agreed. "I understand."

"Can you juggle your workload to get this done?

Irene frowned. "I think so, but it will mean a delay on my other cases."

"Thank you. I appreciate your get-it-done approach." He paused. "I'm considering hiring another senior investigator. We have some employee savings to use this biennium."

Irene was surprised. She had felt they were understaffed for years, but John had always claimed the budget wouldn't flex that much.

"I wanted to get your read on what that might do to the office."

Irene delayed answering to enjoy another sip of coffee. Offering an underfill opportunity meant a less-qualified worker could apply, and possibly be hired, without the full range of qualifications and degrees usually required. "If you hire as underfill, the new person wouldn't come in with experience."

John had clearly thought of that. "I believe the position will cover emergencies and reduce our backlog. We have enough for the rest of this budget cycle. That will allow someone to get some good experience. I'll list it as limited duration, and we'll see what happens next budget cycle."

Irene had only done minimal budgeting at the governmental level. What John was suggesting was a way to burn through a small amount of personnel cost savings without committing the agency to a permanent course of action. As part of the general operating budget, as opposed to a grant or dedicated funding, the OA was always at the mercy of what the legislature decided. The agency had had to spend their allotted funds within the two-year budget window; they could not carry over funding into the new biennium.

"So?" John prompted. "What do you think."

Irene studied her cup. "I think it will be a good thing for the workload. And there might be some hard feelings among the junior investigators who don't get the position."

"Who do you think would apply?" John wanted to know.

"I'm sure Cara and Peter would apply."

"I don't want to give it to Peter."

Irene blinked in surprise. John wasn't usually so forthcoming. "He can do the work. But I would agree he's not ready for the political side." She shrugged. "Let him put in an application. It's good practice. Then let the interviews sort things out."

"I'm not going to put you on the interview team," John warned.

"Excellent. I've been on the last few. Let someone else share the joy."

"I wanted to be clear."

"I understand. I like Peter, but I don't think he's ready to go solo. But I do think he's ready to be a team lead."

"Lead?"

She continued. "Cara will apply, too. She's ready and has some good experience. If she gets the job, that will leave the lead position open for a while. I think we should move Peter into it."

"Do you think his people skills are up to being a team lead?"

"I think he's ready for a next step."

"Moving around investigators doesn't solve the workload problems."

"Put out the announcement and see what happens. You can always put out another announcement for a temporarily junior investigator."

John groaned. "More interviews."

Chapter 8

After work, Irene walked the gray dog. The dog was learning to avoid pulling, but was enthusiastic about anything that moved: cats, squirrels, leaves, birds. That evening, their pace was brisk.

Her phone rang, and an unfamiliar number came up. Still wearing her Bluetooth, she answered it, expecting a telemarketer. "This is Irene."

"Hi, Irene. This is Gary Boyd. The Assistant DA from Clackamas County. We met about six months ago?"

Irene blinked in surprise, remembering the attractive attorney. "Oh hi, Gary." She paused, not knowing where to take the conversation. "Ah… is there a problem?"

"No. No."

There was an awkward silence. Irene saw the dog lunge for a cat crouched under a nearby car. "No. Leave it," she bellowed, trying to reel the dog in.

"Excuse me?"

"I'm sorry. I have a foster dog, and he's basically uncivilized. I was trying to keep him away from a cat."

"Oh. You foster?"

"Well, this is my first one."

"Are you liking it?"

"So far, so good. He's wild. Progress is slow."

"How is your other dog handling it?" When Irene met Gary last year, he had commented on the dog hair on her skirt and shared that he owned a dog as well. Irene didn't remember telling him anything about Percy, but it was possible.

"Percy, my old dog, died about three months ago," she said gently.

"I'm so sorry. Look, I'd better get to it before I put my foot in my mouth any further." He took an audible breath on the other end of the phone. "Would you like to go to dinner with me?"

If the phone call had been a surprise, this was a shock. "That's sudden," Irene said after a pause.

"I wanted to get the Nicols case closed before I asked you out. When I saw your name on the Schuster matter, I thought I would give you a call."

Irene's thoughts bounced around as they continued the walk. He had been easy to work with during the case, diligent and responsible. He was attractive. In their brief conversations he had come off as intelligent and well informed. Irene knew he had a daughter who did 4-H with their dog, but she had never heard anything about a wife. She had noticed he didn't wear a wedding ring.

"Okay. That sounds nice. I'm coming up that direction next week."

"I'd like to take you out in Salem, if that's okay. On Saturday?"

"Wow. Saturday. A real date."

"Pick you up at seven?"

Irene studied the dog who was preparing to lift his leg on a fence post. "Okay."

****

When they arrived back at the house, Irene got another shock. Angie was waiting with Dave and Mike, her two sons. She was unloading them from the car, and they darted for the house as soon as they were released.

As Irene got closer, she was able to see the intense expression on her sister's face. Irene noted her eye makeup was smudged from tears. "Irene, I need you to take the kids for two hours."

Irene debated enforcing her long-standing boundaries about this kind of thing. But somehow, she sensed that Angie was on the edge. "What happened?"

"There was an accident at the dealership. I'm not sure about the details, but one of the mechanics had his arm cut off."

"Of course you can leave the kids here. But where's Jason?"

"That's a great question," said Angie. "He told me he was going skiing with some friends today. But he left his phone at home. I don't know where he is and can't ask him."

Irene assured her sister she could take the kids, and moments later Angie was pulling out of her driveway.

In the confusion of the moment, Irene hadn't had a chance to formally introduce the boys to the gray dog, or vice versa. Apparently, the boys hadn't seen them on the street and so hadn't seen the dog. Angie hadn't noticed. Irene pondered a plan as she stepped up onto the porch. "Mike. Dave. Come here real quick."

She heard the boys groan, having already got out the video system and started a game.

"It's important," she encouraged.

The boys had left the porch door open and she could see them coming. "Okay, wait there. I want you to meet someone."

With that, she brought the gray dog into view. The boys squealed in delight and started to run forward.

Startled, the dog barked at them. They stopped.

"Guys, this is my new foster dog. Let's give him a moment to get settled."

"What's a foster dog?" Dave called loudly.

The dog was thoroughly stirred up, wagging his tail excitedly. He barked again. Irene wished she could have planned this first meeting. "Let's go into the backyard where you can meet him properly."

Eagerly, the boys headed to the back door. Irene brought up the rear, praising the dog for keeping his attention on her. Once in the backyard, Irene got the boys to sit on the step. Then she lured the dog into a sit. "A foster dog," Irene began, rewarding the dog for a moment of quiet sitting with a small treat, "is a dog that I'm helping find a forever home."

"Why aren't you a forever home?" Dave asked.

"You guys know about dog shelters, right?"

They bobbed their heads vigorously.

"So, this dog came from a shelter, and no one knows much about him. I'm trying to figure out what kind of family he needs and help him learn some good habits so his new family will love him."

"But you're a good home, Aunt Ree. Why can't you keep him forever?"

During this conversation, the dog had relaxed enough to shift onto one hip.

"Guys, I'm going to bring him to meet you. Practice your good dog behavior. Don't look him in the eye. Don't pet him. Let him interact with you."

In the days when she and Percy had attended agility trials, Irene had spent time teaching the boys good canine etiquette. Dog shows were a great place to bring children, but it came with a responsibility. The boys had always done well meeting strange dogs.

They were no different this time. Irene brought the dog forward and he happily lunged toward the boys. Within seconds, the dog was licking them, and the boys were giggling hysterically.

Irene watched this for a moment before she said, "Guys, let's walk him around the yard."

They did that, and soon the dog was dividing his attention between sniffing the grass and watching the boys. When they returned to the steps, Irene sat down between the boys and let the dog off his leash. He sniffed, then went to roll in the grass. When the boys laughed, he came back to lick their faces again. A few minutes later, the dog was lying on the grass panting, and Irene and the boys were able to talk again. "Dave, you asked why I can't keep him forever. I might. But, before I make that decision, I need to make sure he's a good dog."

"He's a great dog," Mike said, already loyal.

Irene laughed. "Fair enough. But not every dog is right for every household. I want to give him a chance to find the best home for him."

The boys looked doubtful.

"We need to take some precautions so he doesn't get too excited and hurt one of you."

"Hurt us?" Dave said skeptically.

"Well, you aren't much bigger than him. And he's a dog bred to herd sheep and cows. When dogs are herding, then can nip to get the animals to move in the right direction. We don't want to give this dog a chance to do that to you. We need to teach him to respect you and enjoy little boys as people, not animals to be herded." Irene smiled. "Though we all know you are animals."

On cue, the boys made animal noises. This was a familiar game.

"So, when we go in the house, we need to walk, not run."

They bobbed their heads vigorously.

"I'm going to set up a big cage for him so he can relax. When he's in there, don't bother him. That's his space."

They bobbed their heads vigorously.

"Okay. What should we order for dinner?"

As the boys told her their dinner suggestions, Irene put the dog back on leash and they moved into the house. Within five minutes, the dog was set up in a large exercise pen in the living room, his kennel, bed, and water dish inside with him. Irene ordered Thai and they passed the time finishing the video game the boys had started.

The dog had watched their actions intently, but had settled onto his dog bed, eyes and eyebrows darting expressively as he studied them, but much more relaxed.

The doorbell rang, which upset the dog. Irene chose to ignore the barking, and moved to the door, expecting Angie. It hadn't even been two hours, but maybe things had resolved quickly.

Instead, it was Jason. Sulky and angry. "Boys, let's go," he said tersely.

Mike and Dave had been flopped over the back of the couch to see who had arrived. At their father's order, they sullenly began finding their backpacks and other items. The exchange was so unusual that Irene wasn't sure what was going on. The dog continued to bark, so she went over to ask him to quiet down. Once settled, she turned back to Jason who lurked at the door. His expression was thunderous. Irene searched for something to say. "Did Angie find out what happened to the injured worker?"

"I don't know."

And with that, the boys filed past him. Jason slammed the door shut, leaving Irene bewildered. "Thanks for babysitting, Irene," she mocked to herself, looking at the dog.

He wagged his tail in response.

\*\*\*\*

Irene received Fallbrook's financial records, board minutes, and other required filings Thursday afternoon. It didn't surprise her to find Phyllis Dixon to be a competent bookkeeper. The records were well kept and easy to follow. She took advantage of the accounting program to keep scans of higher dollar amount transactions. Each month was closed promptly and the financial statements sent to the board with several days to spare. Journal entries were meticulous and detailed. Income streams were documented by funding source, a requirement for the federal grants.

Gene Schuster had not mentioned any grants during his initial interview. Irene made a note to follow up with the school board to see if they had reviewed the grants before submission or had any reporting requirements after the program started.

Candace was still out sick. Before falling ill, she and Irene had connected and decided to talk to Fallbrook's board chair, Katie Maldonado, before conducting additional interviews. Irene had set up a video conference for Thursday afternoon, expecting Candace to be available. When she wasn't, Irene decided to move forward.

After grabbing a cup of coffee, she sat down with her laptop in a small conference room. She didn't have to wait long. A few moments later, Katie's profile requested to join the meeting. Irene accepted and saw an attractive older woman of Hispanic descent. She was dressed in a warm fleece jacket, red flannel shirt, and jeans. She wore glasses, but no makeup, and her short black hair was peppered with white. She peered suspiciously at her laptop screen. "Hello Ms. Maldonado," Irene began.

"Call me Katie. You're Irene?"

"Yes."

"*Muy bien.* Now tell me what's wrong."

Irene was taken aback by her directness. "Okay. I'm assuming you have been informed that Phyllis Dixon—"

"Hmph."

Irene continued, "—has filed a formal complaint for wrongful termination. She has also made allegations that there were unusual accounting and program practices going on at Fallbrook."

"Yes. I know. That one. Old sourpuss. Never happy. Making trouble. And then, when she doesn't get her own way, *ay-ay-ay.*"

"I take it you don't think there is anything to her complaints?"

"No."

Irene studied her notes. "Well, let's get started. As you know, I'm with the Oregon Office of Adjudication. I won't have anything to do with the decision on the unfair termination suit. I'm more interested in the financial matters."

Katie made a *pfts* sound. "There are no financial matters unless she caused them."

Irene decided not to pursue that right now. "I'd like to hear about your impression of the termination incident. It might help me understand the context for events."

Katie made a face. "I never liked Phyllis." She said the name with an unaffected tone that was worse than a sneer. "She was always complaining about someone or something. The children. The grounds. How much things cost. Maintenance. Water wasn't wet enough."

Irene gestured encouragement for her to continue.

"And she had to know every little thing. She would snoop. I saw her, once, listening outside Gene's office while he talked to another teacher. She said she was looking for a file, but it's hard to look when there is no file cabinet nearby."

Katie huffed in disapproval, then continued. "There was this girl, we all knew about her. *Muy nerviosa.* I signed many reports about her. But she was in a new program, working with sheep for the fiber program. I hadn't seen her name in weeks. Gene told me he thought she had 'turned a corner.' Then—" Katie's lips tightened, and she paused to compose herself.

"I did not see it. But my friend Maria's daughter was here, working outside." She made a face. "Children. They are not the smartest. The girl, she was working with the sheep and tried to shut the gate behind her. One of the lambs got out. As she—the girl—chased him, the whole herd got out. Then, she chased the herd. They ran through the greenhouse and tore through the other end. A teacher saw and helped get the sheep back into the pen, but by this time the girl was hysterical. Another teacher

91

was trying to calm her down when Phyllis came out and started screaming. She grabbed the girl and shook her. Then the girl slapped Phyllis and called her a name."

Katie shook her head. "Oh, that was too much. Phyllis was determined. Nothing would do but that the girl was expelled and her parents paid for the damage to the buildings. Gene came out and sent the student to the nurse, then told Phyllis to meet him in his office. Mary Pat at the front desk told me that you could hear Gene and Phyllis arguing clear down the hall."

"And the next morning?" Katie continued, slapping her hand on the desk. "Gene asked me to come in to sign a termination letter. When I got there, Phyllis was out in the parking lot. I saw her ambush that girl's parents when they arrived. She tried to give them a bill, but Gene came out and stopped it. He told her that they wouldn't pursue damages. It was part of doing business with the kids."

Katie rubbed the back of her neck. "She started screaming about him being fiscally incompetent. She said she should quit rather than trying to cover up his problems. And good riddance. We did not have a chance to give her the termination letter."

"That's sad."

"I feel sorry for the girl," Katie confessed.

Irene signaled her sympathy. "Do you know if she is okay?"

"Gene told me her grades dropped, again. And she wanted to transfer, but her parents didn't let her. Gene has got her into that fizz program and she's doing better."

"Remind me what the fizz program is again?" Irene asked, making notes.

"'Find Your Success'. FYS," Katie pronounced the acronym as fizz.

The FYS Program was a voluntary, after-school homework program. The school and the student made a contract, with the student promising to complete their homework and tests, and the school giving them a scholarship up to a thousand dollars per year. At the end of the year, there was a one- or two-week trip that students could join with their scholarship money. The school tried to throw in transportation, lodging, and meals where possible, but admission to museums, historical places, and entertainment was covered by the students' scholarship. In addition to these big trips, the teachers and staff worked to provide activities such as movies and plays throughout the year.

Irene made a note on her computer. "That program is a sore point with Phyllis. Can you tell me about it?"

Katie leaned forward in her chair, fierce in her defense. "That program saved my Manuel. And lots of others. He went to Washington D.C. in sixth grade and Philadelphia in eighth grade. And both times, when he came back, all he could talk about was the statues and the buildings and the museums. He started talking about joining the Navy. Serving this country."

"And that was alright with you?"

"Of course. Now, he tells me that he's been assigned to work in navigation and is already learning a new computer program. And he tells me that it's in demand outside the service. And if he wants, when he gets out, he could go to college. But he says he thinks he will stay in the Navy for a while. He tells me he might be on a submarine crew."

Irene smiled. "It's nice to have options."

"Yes. And if it was up to that Phyllis, it would all have been no. She was always saying, no. No to choices for the kids. No to teachers going to help. Oh, the fuss she made because the teachers were being paid to help after school and then paid extra as team leaders on the trips. What does she think? Teachers do not work for free."

Irene looked over her notes. "Were you involved with the board when your grandson was a student?"

Katie shook her head. "I started on the board six years ago. I became board chair two years ago. I would have volunteered sooner, but Gene said it would be better to wait. No conflict of interest."

"What made you become interested in serving on the board?"

"Manuel. He was going to that Estacada school. *No bueno*. His grades were terrible, and he was hanging out with the wrong people. When Fallbrook opened with this new plan, I took Manuel out and told him that working in the ground would do him good. Gene got him squared away. And when Manuel went back to Estacada for high school, he was a good student." She puffed up with pride. "He graduated and decided to go into the Navy."

Irene smiled. "That's wonderful." She decided to move deeper into the finances. "She—Phyllis—claims the program, including the scholarship money, was paid out of state operating funds. Those kinds of expenses are not eligible for state funds."

For the first time, Katie looked unsure. "I don't know about that. Gene kept a chart and showed how the budget balanced. He had grants for many things. He said something about marking things as extracurricular activities, which they get some money for because of the way the law works."

"Did the board approve the program and the

disbursements?"

"Of course. We looked it over and made a motion for each account."

"Did the board review applications before the school applied for grants?"

As Katie thought about the question, Irene noted a lessening of confidence. "Gene would tell us about what he was applying for, and the board chair would sign. And, of course, he would tell us when we got the grants."

"Do you know what kind of reporting requirements these grants had?"

Katie shook her head, confused. "Reporting?"

"Most grants," Irene explained, "require some reporting about the results of the programs and how the money was spent."

"Ah, yes. I did sign final reports."

Irene added a note to her file. "Did the board review which teachers were getting extra payments?"

"All of them were. All of them worked extra and helped out. Many, many hours. The amount we paid them…" She waved her hand and made a *pfts* sound. "So little."

"Do you remember Phyllis having concerns about the FYS program before her termination?"

Katie agreed she did.

"What was her concern?" Irene coaxed.

Katie rolled her eyes. "As I said, she found many things to complain about. '*No. No. No.*' I did not pay attention to her, so I do not remember the specifics."

"Let's move on," Irene said. "Phyllis said that Gene had a credit card, in his name, that he would loan out to the teachers. He'd get the receipts and turn them over to her for reimbursement."

Katie kept her face blank.

Irene continued, "She said it was an airline miles card, so he was receiving fringe benefits. The courts have ruled, in cases like this, that this is inappropriate. The cardholder is unduly enriched by using state funds."

"So many rules," Katie murmured. "And this one, I did not know about. Gene said that it was hard to use the 'official' method because it took so long. He said this was a card for the special purpose. That it provided points that he could use to help the children."

"Records show he put tens of thousands on the card."

"School is expensive. It does not surprise me," Katie said dismissively.

"But the board knew about this," Irene clarified.

"Yes. He told us. He also said that it was for emergencies. Things that were time sensitive or too hard to create a purchase order for—he called them POs. He said companies make it difficult to purchase things using that PO process."

"What is your understanding of how things are usually purchased?" Irene asked.

"A teacher or other faculty would say they needed something. If it was in the budget, the office would create a purchase order. Gene could approve PO's up to five thousand dollars. After that, it needed a second approval, from me or another officer."

"Did you sign many PO's?"

Katie shook her head. "Only a few a month. Maybe one or two."

"What about normal reimbursements?"

Katie looked confused. "What do you mean?"

"When the staff goes out of town for sports or

chaperone duties, do they submit for some kind of reimbursement?"

Comprehension swept across Katie's face. "Ah. Yes. We reimburse for meals, lodging, and mileage when they attend training or sports events where they need to spend the night. We talked about making a limit, but there wasn't a problem. The teachers had receipts and filled out the forms."

Irene made another note. "What about the items being lent out to the community?"

"There is no issue," Katie said impatiently. "The school is part of the community. Why would we ask the people who pay for the items to pay for them again? If someone needs chairs, they sign them out. If someone needs to use the shop, he only asks they leave it clean and if they could donate some time with the children."

"Phyllis says items were lent out and didn't come back. Is that true?"

Katie scoffed. "The school keeps records. What was lent out and when it was returned."

"You mentioned chairs or using the shop. What about," Irene consulted her list, "a leaf blower or a table saw?"

"Neither the board or Gene would have a problem with this." She paused, then said thoughtfully, "Though I did not realize all those school items were being lent out."

"Who would know the most about this?"

"Drew Tungas, the custodian."

They covered a few more details before signing off. Katie finished with, "Gene is not devious, as Phyllis says, but he is ambitious," she confided, shaking her finger. "He writes of 'his program' in a publication. He gives a workshop at a big convention. He is a 'cool customer' but I could tell he was excited. I worried about him leaving the school, not imaginary money schemes."

Chapter 9

Saturday evening, Gary Boyd arrived at Irene's house promptly at seven. Irene was waiting outside on the porch. The gray dog was tucked up inside the house in a kennel as she didn't want to give him a chance to overreact to a new visitor. He had been doing well with exercise and attention, but Irene wasn't ready to introduce him to strangers. That would be an entire training session, which she didn't have time for right then.

She had met Gary when they worked together on a city embezzlement case six months before. They hadn't spent a lot of time together, but Irene had been attracted to his intelligent and thoughtful demeanor. He was around forty with receding sandy-blond hair, cropped short around features that didn't stand out.

She stepped off the porch, Gary opened the passenger side door for her, and let her get settled before closing it again. Once again, she noticed he was missing a leg because the metal of his prosthetic ankle was visible when he moved.

Once he was inside the car, she asked, "Where did you decide we should go?"

"Well, I hope it's not too casual, but the last time I was in town I went to this place called *Vinto's*. They had good food and a nice interior."

"That's a great place," Irene confirmed.

"I wasn't sure what kind of restaurants people use for dates anymore." He laughed awkwardly. "It's been so long."

Irene smiled in sympathy. "Me neither. At least at this one we'll know we can get some good food."

He laughed nervously. "I hate eating in front of someone new because I'm such a picky eater."

"Oh? What don't you like?"

"Well, for starters, I'm allergic to celery."

"Really?"

"Yeah. My dad was too. If I eat more than a bite, I break out into hives."

"Wow. I hadn't heard that one before. I was expecting you to say you were gluten intolerant or a vegan or something."

"I can only dream of having such sophisticated culinary problems. There are things I don't like."

She agreed. "Me too."

Irene saw his smile flash in the dark car interior. "What don't you eat?"

"Well, I don't usually reveal this to strangers," she cautioned playfully.

"I'll never tell," he said. "Scout's honor."

"Were you a Boy Scout?"

He shook his head. "Nope."

Irene smiled. "My deepest, darkest culinary secret is that I loathe tomatoes."

"That's a strong word."

"*Loathe* them," she emphasized.

With an affected shudder, Gary kept the conversation going. "Kale gives me the creeps."

"Kale?"

"It's supposed to be all healthy, right? But have you

ever tried to cut it up and eat it? It's like leather. Far too sturdy for a leafy vegetable. It has clearly got a dark purpose."

Irene agreed. "I'm not sure about any of those leafy things. Take cabbage. It's clearly too compact to be natural."

"No," Gary said in mock dismay. "Don't tell me the cabbage is evil, too."

"I can't stand it. I won't eat sauerkraut. I check egg rolls to make sure they aren't stuffed with it. And I won't eat a salad if it comes with those little purple cabbage ribbons on the side."

"But cabbage is so… round. What do you think it's plotting?"

"That's the point. It's round and can go places. A herd of them will surround our cities and that will be it." Irene snapped her fingers. "No more potatoes."

"Why would they eliminate potatoes?" Gary asked.

"Because everyone likes them."

"Lots of people like cabbage. I mean, think of those dolls—"

Irene shuddered dramatically. "Do not get me started on those. Talk about evil. Only that show about a house on the prairie matches the sheer deviousness."

"You are against the little house?" Gary asked in confusion. "My sister would have hated you. She loved that show."

"So did the meanest girl in my class. I took a vow never to willingly watch that show."

Gary thought about it. "Fair enough. Any other food issues I should be aware of?"

"How long have you got?"

They continued in this general manner throughout

the drive, waiting for their table, and getting settled. When the waiter revealed the special was *sukuma wiki*, African braised kale with tomatoes, they both burst out laughing. The waiter left them to review the menu, glad to get away.

Within fifteen minutes, they had ordered, and the conversation had turned to work. Each of them worked in a form of law enforcement, so they told some stories before returning to the prosecution of the city worker who had embezzled hundreds of thousands of dollars.

"It's a shame she only got eighteen months in minimum security," Gary said.

"Judges won't crack down on white collar crimes."

The appetizers arrived, and while they were nibbling on the various cheese delicacies, Irene changed the subject. "How is your daughter's 4-H project going this year?" Irene knew that Gary's daughter owned a Golden retriever that she showed in 4-H as well as some AKC events.

"She's coming right along. This year she's focusing on getting Layla's trick title."

"That nice. I like that the AKC is focusing so much on bringing in new performance events."

"Me too, though I wonder if it might be better to contract them out. AKC runs great conformation shows, but the activities can feel like an afterthought."

"True."

"How's your new foster dog doing?" Gary asked conversationally. "Any chance for a foster failure?"

Irene thought about it. "Let's just say I'm leaving room for the possibility. For right now, I'm working on civilizing him." She recounted the story of his capture. Gary laughed.

Irene decided to pry. "Do you have full custody of your daughter?"

"Yes. My ex-wife lives in Las Vegas."

"That's a long way away. What does she do?"

"She a corporate medical lawyer. We met in law school. I went with what interested me, she went for what would get her money and position."

Irene studied him. "Are you bitter about that?"

Gary shrugged. "I was for a while after the divorce, but I realized that those differences had been there right from the start with us. I fell in love with an ambitious, politically-minded woman who was interested in the world of commerce. That never changed. We got married. We had a daughter and a house and all the rest. But fundamentally, that's who she was. One day she told me she had applied for her dream job and got it. I was excited for her. She'd be the VP of the legal department in one of the nation's largest health care conglomerates. Then she told me it was in Las Vegas and that she didn't want to be married anymore."

"That simple?"

He shrugged and tilted his hand in a so-so gesture. "Probably not. It was hard. I asked her to stay. I offered to move. But in the end, I think she saw the situation more clearly than I did. She wasn't happy and was prepared to take whatever steps she felt were necessary to improve things. In her eyes, it was as simple as the out clause on a contract that wasn't working. I stayed here. This was what I wanted."

Gary's story disturbed her in that he hadn't cared enough to fight for his marriage. She mentally shrugged her shoulders. How much could she expect in a five-minute summary?

"What about you?" Gary asked, twirling pasta onto his fork.

"Nothing to tell. I've never been married."

"Lived with someone?"

"Nope."

"Engaged?"

"Uh-uh."

"Wow. A bona fide virgin."

Irene guffawed. "I wouldn't go that far. I was involved with a man for about three years, but that ended two years ago. Since then, a lot has been going on. Work." She hesitated, "Some health challenges. Dating hasn't been a high priority item."

"Do you mind if I ask about the health challenges?"

Irene paused. "I don't mind, but I don't want to spend the rest of dinner discussing them. Let's just say that they are chronic and long term. I'm working on getting stable."

"Any chance it's MS?" Gary asked. "My cousin has that. She talks about it the same way."

Irene looked at him in surprise. "Well, actually, yes."

"That's nasty. She has special food and exercise. A medication regime. It takes up a lot of her time. How are you doing with it?"

"About the same. The last few months have been good. I hate to admit it, but not having a dog slowed down my life, which helped."

Gary smiled. "There is no way that being dogless could have improved anything. You are obviously mistaken."

"Could be," Irene admitted with an answering smile. "There's a first time for everything."

They ate in silence for a few minutes.

Gary finished chewing a bite. "You haven't asked about my leg," he pointed out.

Irene blinked in surprise. "Well, it doesn't seem like that would be polite."

He smiled. "It's part of me and somewhat unusual. I prefer to get it out in the open. And I have some good stories about my recovery."

She nodded but was still unsure. "What would you like to tell me about your leg?"

"Most people want to know how I lost it."

"I'd listen if you want to tell me."

Again, he smiled. "After high school, I joined the army. I ended up serving in Afghanistan. We were on patrol when our truck got stuck. We got out to fix it. The truck ended up rolling and my leg was crushed."

"That must have been awful."

He nodded. "It was. And the physical therapy afterward was no joke. I'm really lucky the wound healed so well. I have friends who still struggle with their injuries."

"I've heard stories," Irene said.

"The hardest part," he admitted, "was developing a new body image. I played sports all through high school and college. When I went into the army, I was in great shape, which helped. And suddenly, everything was different. My body didn't move the same way. I felt ugly."

Irene covered his hand with hers.

"I told you about my marriage. My ex-wife told me she didn't care about my leg, which is one of the things that attracted me. I know she was aware of it. Sometimes she'd fuss about something I was doing, asking if it was safe. But I never asked her if my amputation didn't matter to her or if it was something that made her feel sorry for me."

He paused to move a crumb around his plate. "Then when we divorced… well, a lot of stuff was said. I've been working through some of it with a counselor. But you hadn't mentioned it, and I feel self-conscious about it."

Irene squeezed his hand. "I am sorry for your pain. And I'm sorry for making it worse." She thought about it. "I guess I fall into the 'don't care' camp. Obviously, losing a leg is painful, but I've always found intelligence and behavior more attractive than looks." She smiled at him. "Colonel Brandon over Willoughby."

He laughed. "Do I need to worry about my age, as well?"

"No. On that we're equal." She studied his face for a moment. "I empathize with losing your leg. I worry about ending up in a wheelchair due to the MS."

"Is that why you're not sure about keeping your foster dog?" Gary asked.

Irene looked down at the remainder of her rice bowl. "I don't know. It's complicated to think about it all right now."

Gary met her eyes. He was a good listener. "What's complicated about now?" he asked gently.

Irene broke their gaze. "I'm not sure." She took another bite and chewed. Gary watched her patiently. She swallowed and admitted, "I can't tell if I'm having trouble moving forward or simply taking some time to breathe."

"It's good to take your time and not jump into things."

"Yes," Irene agreed.

His eyes met hers again. "But it's possible to be too cautious," he said.

Gary insisted on paying for dinner, so Irene invited him to *Gerry's Cake Place* for dessert. They sat in the well-lit diner for a while, sharing a piece of chocolate layer cake.

"In a few weeks," Gary began, "my daughter is doing to take the dog to a big show down in Albany. Would you like to hang out with us for a day trip?"

Irene paused, then forked up another bite. "I need to check my calendar before I can commit."

Gary studied her. "Are you reluctant because you think you'll have a conflict? Or for some other reason?"

Irene laughed in surprise. "You are so direct. I thought all lawyers were crafty and liked to trick people into confessions."

"Tom-a-to, to-ma-to." He put down his fork and waited.

Irene studied the remaining cake on the plate before saying, "Gary, there's a lot going on with me. I don't know if I can add a romantic relationship right now."

"Ah-ha," he said with a dramatic waggle of his eyebrows. "You think I'm romantic."

Irene smiled, but kept her expression serious, unwilling to soften for something this important. "Yes."

He studied her. "Irene, I also have a lot going on. Going on a second date is not exactly a commitment. It's just a second date. The one I am proposing involves a thirteen-year-old, a building full of dogs, and maybe lunch from a dicey vendor. It's not a trip to Acapulco."

Irene smiled. "Well, I can't be too careful. As a lawyer, I'm sure you would agree I should always read the fine print."

****

After Irene returned home, the dog sniffed her thoroughly. They walked around the block happily enough, but after they returned, he didn't want to settle in his play area. He sat on his dog bed and stared at her, occasionally making a soft whine. Irene tried taking him out in the backyard several more times, but when that did not appear to be his problem, Irene decided to take him on another quick walk.

On previous nights, when she settled the dog into his crate for the night, he had dropped off quickly. This evening, he stared at her as she brushed her teeth, then started to whimper when she turned off the light. Irene took him outside again, then returned him to his crate. He whined. Irene checked him thoroughly to make sure he didn't have a hidden injury. He happily waved his tail but showed no sign of distress. She put him back in his kennel, turned out the light, and he whined. Irene decided to read for a few minutes. He sat in his kennel, watching her intently. Irene looked back.

He was not a cuddly dog. He enjoyed a belly rub, food, or a good walk. Toys, including ball and tug were awesome. He rarely wanted to sit right next to her when he was under supervised freedom in the house. Instead, he would sniff the corners, find a toy, then settle up on the furniture.

Irene let him out of the crate to see what would happen. He followed her back to her chair and when she sat down to continue reading, lifted his front half into her lap. Irene caressed his ears for a while, then turned to her book. He leaped up into the chair and curled up in the remaining tiny space.

108

She was tired and anxious to get to sleep, but the dog was working something out. She budgeted a half hour before she would try to settle him again. To her surprise, a few minutes later, he unfolded himself from the chair, shook, and returned to his kennel where he lay down, clearly signaling he was ready to relax.

Irene shut the kennel door, climbed into bed, and turned off the light.

****

Sunday morning, Irene met her best friend, Sharon, at Minto Brown for a walk. Sharon's life partner, Carrie Daugherty, said hello to her briefly before starting a marathon-training run.

Minto Brown Island Park was an elaborate, lovely park with miles of trails, an enormous off-leash dog area, and great nature viewing. Considered the crown jewel of the Salem Park system, it was adored by all recreation users. Sharon and Irene had decided to forgo off-leash play because the gray dog wasn't allowed to be in a dog park. Even if they had been inclined to try, Irene didn't know what his recall might be like and remembered the goose chase. Another factor: Sharon's dog, Mule, could be a picky playmate.

When Irene and Sharon introduced the dogs, they hit it off immediately. Mule hadn't always liked her old dog, Percy. When they had first met, Percy had lifted his lip to tell the younger Mule not to mess with him and Mule had never forgot it. The foster dog and Mule smelled each other, agreed to some arrangement, and moved off. Sharon and Irene followed them.

"So, how did your big date go?" Sharon asked.

"You and Gary should meet. You have the same element of subtleness."

"Good to know. Answer the question," Sharon demanded.

Irene shrugged. "It was very nice. We had a nice meal, we laughed, we talked about life stories. Basic first date stuff."

"Are you going to see him again?"

"He asked me to go to the Albany show with him and his daughter."

"Are you going to go?"

"I don't know. I'm not sure I'm in the right place for a relationship."

"Pfft. Right place. As if." There was a two-second pause. "You should go."

"I am shocked you think that," Irene said dryly, anything but shocked. "Your opinion is duly noted."

They walked another quarter mile in silence, watching the dogs sniff all the things.

Sharon blurted out, "Are you going to keep Max?"

"Why don't you tell me?" Irene said. It wasn't sarcastic. Irene was interested in her opinion.

"I think you should. He's a nice dog."

"I'm nervous about his energy level."

"You were nervous about Percy's energy level."

"That was fifteen years ago and before MS."

"So?"

Irene was silent for a moment before answering. Sharon was her best friend and probably her most valuable health advocate. As the owner of Hands to Soul Healing Center, Sharon had supported her diagnosis by offering MS-specific yoga class and other resources. Sharon was also bossy. Irene didn't mind the trait, and even valued it occasionally, but Sharon's freedom with her opinions sometimes made her feel cornered.

She admitted. "I've been having some numbness with all this new walking."

Sharon stopped. "Do we need to stop?"

"No. I'm fine right now. I like him, and I think he has potential. But I'm not sure I can handle him long-term."

For once, Sharon was silent for a while. "If you decided to keep him, maybe hiring a dog walker would be a good move. Or taking him to a doggy day care."

"I don't know. A dog walker seems silly. I mean, why have a dog if you aren't going to walk him?"

"In order to have a dog and keep yourself sound."

"Sound," Irene said in disgust. "I'm not a horse."

"Same principle."

"Doggie day care is so expensive."

"You're a cheapskate."

"What's your point?"

Sharon gave her a stern look. "Don't say no without considering the options. That goes for this second date as well."

Irene snorted. "Second date. Why aren't there better terms for these things when you're my age?"

"It's a conspiracy," Sharon said. "Don't you get the newsletter? *Conspiracies Against Women Quarterly.*"

Irene snorted in laughter.

As another set of dog walkers passed in the opposite direction, the women concentrated on keeping their dogs quiet and focused. Once the trail was clear again, Irene said, "Jason came to my house last week. By himself. He said he wanted to talk."

"That's weird." Sharon had met the various members of Irene's family and knew of her brother-in-law.

Irene agreed. "I thought so, too."

"What did he want to talk about?" Sharon asked.

"Angie and their situation."

Sharon looked nonplused. "That seems like a stretch."

"I know. It was bizarre."

"Do you think something is up with them?"

Irene thought about it. "Obviously, something is. I mean, with Angie's new job offer and all." She paused. "But this seems like something else."

"Do you think she'll take the promotion and move to Bend?" Sharon asked.

"I think she wants to do it, but Jason apparently isn't excited about it."

"Why not?"

Irene shrugged impatiently. "I guess he feels like he should be the breadwinner or some other macho crap."

A squirrel crossed the path, exciting the dogs. The dogs bounded over to the tree it had climbed. Irene and Sharon hauled them away from the tree and up the path.

"I hope this doesn't blow up," Irene said.

"You know it will," Sharon said sarcastically. "Life has been too quiet for too long. If Angie doesn't wreck something, Jennifer will."

Irene agreed but felt the need to defend her family. "Weren't you the person advising me to adopt an untrained dog and accept a second date? You like drama."

Sharon snorted. "I like *your* drama. You're entitled. Angie and Jennifer have had enough drama to last a lifetime. They shouldn't get any more."

Chapter 10

Monday morning, Irene arrived at the state motor pool to meet Candace and drive up to Fallbrook. They had made plans to leave Salem at seven in the morning and would interview Fallbrook teachers, staff, and board members for the entirety of the work day.

Minutes ticked by, and Irene didn't see Candace. She finally thought to take out her work phone and turn it on. The icon for a voicemail message appeared within seconds.

*"Irene, it's Candace. I'm afraid I can't make it to work this morning. We're all still under the weather. Call me so we can schedule a different day."*

Irene closed her eyes, then opened them to look up at the dark morning sky. A touch of pink was beginning to show on the horizon, but the stars were still visible.

She rubbed her neck and continued to stare at the sky above her.

She and Candace had reviewed the Fallbrook financial records but found nothing out of order. The numbers appeared in line with other districts of the same size, with Fallbrook being thriftier than average in areas such as maintenance, sports, and general supplies. Most of the overages were in teacher salaries, not uncommon due to contract and budgeting variables. The school appeared to be breaking even, and the accounting provided a good representation of financial position.

Before falling ill, Candace had discussed interview strategies with Irene.

"We'll divvy up the interviews," she'd said. "Keep them short. Get an overview of things in general but focus on reimbursements and the afterschool programs."

Irene had agreed. Certain monies were allowed to be spent in certain ways. If they weren't, that created a problem. "If there is a problem, it will be in expense allowability and reimbursement procedures."

Candace had drawn a large banner on her notes. "Do you think we should ask questions about Phyllis? Try to find out more information about her termination?"

Irene had paused, considering. "No. She's a problem, but I don't think she's *our* problem. I'm inclined to tell people we're focusing on the financial parts and keep out of the human resource aspects. We already know there was a personality clash between her and Schuster. Why get more details?"

"Maybe she's the source of the financial issues."

"What makes you say that?"

Candace had shrugged. "It isn't that I've spotted anything. But if we ask questions, we might discover something."

Now, considering this previous conversation, Irene dropped her gaze and reached for her phone again. She made a call to her boss, John Fisher, explaining what had happened and making several suggestions for moving forward.

After he agreed. Irene clicked off her phone, then got behind the wheel to begin the long drive to Fallbrook.

****

Irene set up in the staff lounge to work through the interviews. Without Candace there to assist, Irene had to hurry each interview. Teachers and other staff members filed in to answer questions, defending Gene and disparaging Phyllis, whether asked or not.

The first interview that Irene considered significant was with Martin "Marty" Swanson, the science teacher. Marty operated an after-school program focused on robotics as well as led a vigorous biology program that integrated with the farming ventures. His name was also sprinkled liberally on the reimbursement ledgers. Marty arrived on schedule. Irene shook his hand, then they sat at the plastic cafeteria table across from each other.

"Thank you for meeting me, Mr. Swanson," Irene began.

"Call me Marty," he said with a smile. "I only make the kids call me Mr. Swanson. This sounds like fun. It's my break and I get to hear gossip."

Irene laughed. "Well, I don't know about that. These meetings are short, and we try to keep them focused on money questions."

"Money is gossip, too," Marty said affably.

Irene smiled. "I'm confident you've heard about Phyllis Dixon's accusations about her release from employment as well as abuse of funding in the school. Several investigations have stemmed from those allegations. I'm from the Oregon Office of Adjudication, so my focus is on any funding irregularities and to ensure monies are being spent in accordance with state laws and rules."

"Fair enough," Marty said.

"I'd like to focus on your reimbursements. Over—" Irene looked at her notes "—ten thousand each year for the last five years."

Marty blinked, pausing to consider her suddenly

serious tone. "Well, science can be expensive. I also run an after-school program. It adds up."

Irene checked her notes. " 'Spring into STEM' you call it. What kind of activities does the program host?"

"Well, of course, it depends on the age. We have a different age group each day of the week. The youngest group is simple stuff, but the older kids are involved in a water-quality monitoring program as well as a robotics segment."

Marty shifted forward in his chair, excited to talk about the program. "We break it down into eight-week units, each with its own enrollment option. That allows us some flexibility if things don't appeal to some of the kids or if they have a conflict with sports. Of course, the robotics unit is always popular, but we get good attendance even with the recycling segments."

"It sounds great. Do you have a budget for the program?"

"Yes. Gene makes me write one each year."

"Does he ever change it or make comments?"

"Of course. I always ask for the moon, and he always cuts it way back."

"Where are the funds coming from?"

Marty looked confused. "What do you mean?"

"Has he ever said anything about a grant or what fund he's using to pay for all this?"

Marty shook his head. "It's all marked into after-school programs."

"Why are there so many reimbursed costs? Why don't you order what you need through the public procurement channels?"

"I try, but it can be hard to find the right part in the timeline we need. It's easier and faster to go down and pick up what we need."

"Does anyone have to approve your purchases?"

"Gene signs off for anything over two hundred fifty dollars. We'll talk about how things are going a couple times a week, and so he knows when something comes up."

Irene moved on to the next set of questions. "You've gone on each FYS trip for the last eight years. Most of the other teachers I've spoken to have only gone on one or two. Why is that?"

He looked perplexed. "I never thought about it. Gene is in charge of the program, but I guess you could say I'm backup."

"Not Miriam Freeman?" Irene asked.

"Nah." Marty waved his hand. "She works with the businesses and the facilities. But she has a daughter and no one at home to help, so she doesn't stay after school or travel."

Irene made a note. "Tell me about the FYS trips."

"Well, they're designed to be an end-of-the-year treat. The program is strict, so we want it to be worthwhile. We try to pick someplace fun but also educational. We select a theme for the year, civics or ecology or something, that we can tie into the destination. The kids work all year to qualify, and they don't always. But they can save up for the next year's trip. Then we go. We try to schedule a balance between educational stuff and fun items. It's hard because you can't let the kids have free time to themselves, but they do okay."

"It sounds like hard work. Why do you go?"

He laughed. "Crazy, I guess."

"Is your time donated, or do you get paid?"

"I get paid, but Gene always makes sure I get at least a couple of nights off, so I get a chance to do some sightseeing."

"What about other expenses?"

He shrugged, unconcerned. "The school pays for my room and plane. I get an allowance for meals and such. If I do something on my free time, I pay for it, of course."

"Does Gene collect your receipts?"

"Of course." Marty studied her as though she were crazy for asking such a basic question.

"What about the kids? I understand they receive some spending money."

He inclined his head. "The spending money is earned, like the rest of the expenses, throughout the year by participating in the programs and meeting the target goals."

"Does Gene collect all those receipts?"

"Well, the lodging and admissions are paid for ahead of time. The kids don't need much, but we allow ten dollars a day for each kid to have something in their pocket." He looked thoughtful for a moment. "I don't think we collect those receipts. Mostly the kids buy a souvenir or a candy bar. It's not a lot of money."

"How about your trip expenses?"

"Gene has always given me a credit card which I use if something comes up."

"Was the credit card in your name? His name? The school's name?"

He looked blank. "It must have been in my name, or I couldn't have signed for things."

"But you don't remember?"

"I don't."

"And Gene would collect those receipts?"

"Yes," he repeated the affirmation, again displaying his utter disbelief she would ask.

"Another teacher told me that Gene asked her to pay out of pocket, then request reimbursement."

Marty shook his head. "That happened the first year, but I don't think it's happened since. In fact, now that I think about it, the last few years he's given us credit cards with the district name on them. We turn in receipts at the end of the trip."

****

Next, Irene interviewed the school librarian, Georgina Ortega. After a few pleasantries, which Irene tried to push along in the interest of time, she asked her first question. "Do you do the ordering for the library?"

Georgina nodded. Irene waited, but the other woman did not expand on the topic.

"What is the library budget?" Irene nudged.

"One hundred fifty thousand with my salary and all the other costs."

Irene checked her notes. "That's not much."

"Gene tells me, write a big budget and we can see. Then he cuts it down. He says he wants to see what I can dream up. He says big ideas don't come from a limited budget. Then he says we have to work with reality."

Irene smiled encouragingly. "That sounds frustrating."

Georgina made a dismissive gesture. "Gene lets me explore the possibilities. And he always listens to me. As long as I stay in the budget, he lets me manage the library. Doing budget paperwork is not a problem."

"How do you make purchases?" Irene asked.

"About once a month I make an order to the suppliers. Replacements or new books. I always try to make sure that we aren't ordering too many times, because shipping is expensive."

"What's the size of a usual order?"

"During the year, maybe a thousand dollars. Over the summer, I put in a large order of about ten thousand."

"What is the ordering procedure?" Irene asked, taking notes.

"We have a couple of main suppliers. I make a purchase order and give it the business manager. That used to be Phyllis Dixon. She would get it approved, then send it to the vendor."

"What if it's a small item?"

"I have to get a PO for anything over a hundred dollars. If it's under that, I can purchase it and ask for reimbursement. But I don't like to do that."

"Why not?" Irene asked.

She made a face. "I am afraid that Phyllis will deny it."

"Why?"

"She was always picking apart my orders, asking if things were 'necessary'." Georgina said the word as though it burned her tongue. "And then, she delayed making the order. By the time things arrived, sometimes the kids were not interested anymore."

"Can you give me an example?"

"The kids, they love *manga* and *anime*." Irene had a blank moment. Apparently, it showed on her face, because Georgina explained, "You know, those Japanese comics.

Irene nodded, able to place the term. "Oh, yeah."

"I try to keep track of what is coming out and order the books and videos," Georgina continued. "They even have these apps we can put on the tablets for learning to draw them and such. Phyllis said they weren't 'necessary' but Gene had signed the purchase order so what did she care? I saw that purchase order in her box for three weeks before I went to Gene. He made her process it."

"Do you ever send your orders out for bid?" Irene inquired.

"Not often. I try to use the state procurement system. They have a contract with several library services. The only bid I ever had to go through was for setting up the computer system, and that was for the whole school."

"Is that the only time that you put something out for bid?" Irene asked.

"Almost everything is on the state price agreements, so I can simply fill out a PO. My orders are small. It is not complicated."

Irene decided there was nothing else to discover. "Thank you for taking the time to talk to me. I'll let you—"

Georgina interrupted her. "Gene is a good man. Phyllis is a terrible person. She would delay my orders and deny things the kids wanted. She said it was because the budget was tight and people were always making mistakes, but I think it was because she wanted control." She looked up to meet Irene's eyes. "I also wanted to tell you that I overheard Phyllis making a phone call to immigration to report the parents of some of the children."

Shocked, Irene blurted, "Are you sure? That the call was to ICE, I mean?"

Georgina looked down at her hands. "I am sure. I did not tell Gene. Then Gene fired Phyllis, and it didn't seem important. Now, you are here. My husband and I talked about it, and I feel I must report this."

"Tell me what you saw."

"We had high enrollment last fall. Gene was scrambling to find room for an extra classroom and teachers. For a few weeks, one of the classes met in the library projects room."

Irene nodded.

Georgina continued. "The class ended up being an ESL booster for the kids of three families. Thirteen children, first grade to fourth. By Christmas, the children had moved into the grade that matched their age, but Gene started them out here to give them a chance to get used to things.

"I could tell the parents were undocumented. They were obviously poor. They didn't want to come into the school." She paused. "My parents were undocumented. From Mexico. I could recognize the signs."

Again, Irene nodded.

"The kids had been attending for a few weeks, and then Phyllis started coming by in the mornings." Georgina rolled her eyes. "She almost never left her office until all the kids were in their classrooms. But suddenly, she started coming around with offers to help these teachers with roll calls or copying tests.

"I couldn't figure it out. It was so unlike her. She never helped with anything. Then I saw her use her phone to take a picture of one of the kid's papers. I asked her what she was doing. I guess I scared her, and she dropped her phone. She grabbed at it, but I saw 'ICE' as the caller. She said there was a discrepancy between the name he was using and the office paperwork. But she didn't handle enrollment. Chick is the only one who does. The teachers can get records, but they have to go through the registrar. I was going to mention the incident to Gene."

"ICE could be In Case of Emergency," Irene pointed out.

Georgina shook her head. "I thought about that. But two days later, ICE raided a local farm and two of the kids had their fathers picked up."

Realizing her eyes were watering, Irene blinked.

Georgina continued, her eyes cold. "Two days later, Phyllis was fired. I've told the story to Gene. He believes me but says there isn't much to do now that she is gone. ICE targets the farms around here. Even if ICE doesn't come to the school, attendance has dropped. Parents don't trust us with their children."

By now, Georgina was crying as well. "I loved the library when I was growing up. I wanted the kids here to feel the same thing. But she has ruined it."

****

Irene's next interview was with Andrew "Drew" Tungas, the head of maintenance. Irene had high hopes for this interview; support staff knew everything. Andrew arrived a couple minutes late, jogging into the cafeteria to make up time. He was lean and nimble, with short dreadlocks held back from his middle-aged features. They went through the introductory ritual, including permission to use first names. Drew spoke in a quiet voice influenced by his Jamaican birth. Irene explained her interest, and Drew listened.

"Phyllis is bad news," he said, shaking his head.

"Why do you say that? Did you have a problem with her?"

"No problem," he said slowly. "I simply didn't like her. She was always sneaking around. Never say what she was after."

"Okay. Tell me about what you do here at the school."

He smiled. "You name it."

Irene smiled back. "Give me an average day."

"Well, today, I got here at six and opened up the school. I checked on the animals. I checked the irrigation lines and the greenhouse temperatures. Then I came inside to check the security cameras and such. We have a couple of night guys to do the cleaning and basic janitorial. By seven, I was working on the repair list. When the kids start arriving, I make sure to go out where they can see me."

"Why?"

"Some of them want to say hi. Some want to ask questions. Some want to get in trouble. If I'm out where they can see me, things go more smoothly."

"Okay. What next?"

"More repairs. Line up bids for the bigger jobs. And I'm out on the grounds, helping with the plants and such. It keeps me busy."

"Several people have mentioned certain repairs and maintenance being delayed."

He shrugged. "It's always a balancing act. The budget can only be stretched so much."

"What kinds of things have been put off?"

He looked thoughtful. "Well, the gym floor is in rough shape. I'd like to prioritize that, but Gene has it a couple years out."

"Why haven't you fixed it?"

Drew shrugged. "I don't have the expertise to repair it, and it's too big for only me. The replacement will cost tens of thousands, and it isn't heavily used. The kids are outdoors as much as possible." He paused for a moment. "If we wanted to do it cheaper, we could. But some kids have that —" He snapped his fingers, searching for the right word. "—sensory overload thing. Gene wants to redo the gym with sound barriers and other things to help reduce the sounds and echoes. They only use it for assemblies." He chuckled. "And Gene tries not to do too many of those."

Irene scribbled a reminder. "Okay. What else has been delayed?"

He thought. "We decided to re-seed the outdoor activity fields. And this last summer we decided to repair the south bathroom stalls rather than replace them."

"Are any of those student safety issues?" Irene asked.

Drew shook his head. "No. Gene would never allow that. Anything having to do with safety or keeping the school running, that's what comes first." Then he shrugged. "His main concern is keeping the building warm and dry, then the outdoor programs."

"Have you had any problems getting money for projects? Or having things paid for?"

He snorted. "Of course. No one ever likes how much things cost. But Gene and I always go over bids together. And if we can't swing it, he'll help brainstorm a solution."

"Give me a for instance."

"Well, going back to the bathroom stalls. Those have been on the summer schedule for the last few years. We had a couple of bids to have the whole system redone last summer, but the bids came in high."

"How high?"

"Well, we budgeted ten thousand for all three

bathrooms, but the bid came in at fifty thousand. So, we talked about it and decided to find something through the state's surplus system. We found enough materials to do two of the bathrooms. But we couldn't find enough to do the south bathroom. So, Gene and I took the stalls apart and refinished them. We had to re-drill all the parts, and it looks clunky, but they have a nice fresh coat of paint on them. They'll hold until we can find more parts."

"You said that you and Gene took the stalls apart?"

"Oh yeah. He's here nearly all summer, working on the projects."

Irene made a note. "The other two maintenance workers are on the night shift?"

"Yes. There are Ian and John. Both of them are through the Goodwill Job Training Program. They don't have great social skills, but they are hard workers."

"So, if they aren't good socially, how do they interact with the children?"

"They don't. They come in after school. They do the garbage and the floors. Clean what needs cleaning. Do anything the cafeteria staff has set out. But they aren't around when the kids are. That's why I make a big point of hanging out when the kids come to school. I don't want those kids thinking that the school is magically taken care of. I want them to know there are people here who do that work. Ian and John can't be here, so I take care of it."

Irene smiled. "That's a great attitude. Are there any kids who you have trouble with?"

"Of course. I mean, they are kids."

"Any in particular?"

"A few. Gene knows about them. A few days on janitor duty sorts them out."

126

"And if it doesn't?"

He looked thoughtful. "Well, a few years ago, we had this one kid. He was a transfer, and he was determined he wouldn't like it here. He set off a few explosions in the bathroom, tagged a couple of walls, carved his name in a desk. Gene took him on as a project. He started assigning him out in the fields. I mean, all the time. Almost never in the classroom. That kid was so tired, he didn't know which way was up. And, of course, he didn't have any energy to dream up problems. After a while, Gene started moving him back into the classrooms for an hour or two. I don't think he ever got to being in the classrooms all day, but he was there for a while. The thing was, I know his grades improved. And I heard that he ended up graduating from Estacada."

"Is that typical of how Gene deals with the difficult students?"

"Yeah. Gene says that kids don't like being cooped up. He has this whole theory about alternative learning and evolution. It gets convoluted. I heard he gave a big speech about it last year."

Irene changed the direction of her questions. "The issue of items leaving the school has come up a couple of times. Do you have any thoughts about that?"

Drew looked wary. "What do you mean?"

"The school functions like an open campus. The parents and community are allowed to check out tables and chairs, or work in the shop. Have you had any problems with that?

He frowned. "It's not my favorite part of the job, but I can see why Gene wants to let it happen."

"Why is it not your favorite part of the job?"

"It's extra work, keeping track of things, calling and

reminding people to bring things back, repairing or cleaning things. And it's all but impossible to get the school gates closed at a decent hour because there is almost always someone here doing something."

"Like what?"

"Well, Marty has been doing a robotics project this term. So, the kids come in after school and use the shop to make the robots. A couple of them have some state contest they want to enter. Some of the parents come by after they get out of work to help. Someone has to stick around to put things away, turn out the lights, and close the gate."

"Who does that?"

"Marty. He's great at tying up loose ends, but everyone helps out. I hate it when the drama club is going on. They could practice *acting* like they know how to turn off a light."

Irene smiled. "What about people taking things off the grounds? Teachers borrowing equipment? Parents taking tools home?"

He shrugged. "It happens. The school has a lenient policy."

"Does all the equipment have a sign out sheet?"

"Mostly."

"What if someone wants to borrow something not on the list. Like a leaf blower?"

"They check with me, and if we can spare it, I'll have them log it out at the front desk."

"Any problem getting things back?"

He smiled. "Not any more than the usual teeth pulling."

Irene smiled in sympathy. "Is there anything else you'd like to tell me?"

Drew shook his head. "Nope. Gene, he's cool. But Phyllis is bad news."

Chapter 11

Irene was rinsing out her coffee cup, in preparation for her final hit of the day, when Charlotte "Chick" Roy joined her in the staff lounge. "How are you?" Chick said brightly.

Irene smiled back, remembering how much she had liked this woman upon their initial meeting. "Tired. It's a long day."

Chick nodded. "Didn't you have someone with you?"

Irene shook her head. "Candace, my co-worker, was unable to come today. She and her family have the flu."

Chick's expression morphed into concern. "That's too bad. I guess it's that time of year."

Irene agreed.

"How are things going? Chick continued. "Finding anything?"

Irene smiled. While sometimes people ask questions, trying to discover a secret, most people ask out of politeness. This is what she sensed from Chick. "Not much. It doesn't sound like Phyllis made many friends.

Chick rolled her eyes. "I'm sure you've heard an earful."

Irene agreed. "One thing I want to check on is the borrowing of equipment. No one thinks it's a problem, but the cafeteria workers said that sometimes groups used the tables, and they had to scramble to get them back before lunch."

"That's happened a couple times," Chick agreed. "But it's not common."

"No one I've talked to thinks it's a problem," Irene concurred. "I want to make sure the board knows about the policy." She paused. "There isn't much here. No one liked Phyllis, and she gave some people a hard time. But that's not the kind of thing the OA investigates."

"It would be impossible to investigate every troublemaker," Chick agreed.

****

The board consisted of five members: Katie Maldonado, the board chair; Annie Cummings, the board treasurer; Ava-May Stuart, the board secretary; Joe Floyd, member at large; and Tyler Meadows, member at large.

Irene wanted to interview the group together, with the addition of Gene Schuster. The school only had a few places to hold a group of that size. Irene walked down to the teacher's conference room.

The first board member to arrive was Tyler Meadows, accompanied by Gene. Irene guessed Meadow's age to be mid-thirties. She knew he had children in the school. A second board member, Ava-May Stuart, arrived in tandem with Katie Maldonado, the board chair. Like Katie, Ava was middle aged, but where Katie gave off an air of practical cheerfulness, Ava-May's elegant clothing and handmade bag whispered money.

Joe Floyd, the longest serving board member, arrived next. He was older than Katie by at least twenty years and was wearing a Hawaiian shirt, khakis, and a hat that proclaimed *"Danger! Grumpy Old Man! Proceed with Caution!"* He sat down in the seat next to Gene.

Gene glanced at his phone, scowled, and announced, "Annie will be running late. She'll text me when she gets here."

Irene gathered up her notes. "Alright. Let's get started."

She moved to the front of the room, scowling at the chalkboard adorning the wall. It made her feel like she would have to present a book report or solve a math equation. "Thank you all for making time for me this evening. I believe you are familiar with why I'm here. Does anyone have any questions?"

"Let's get this over with fast," Joe grumbled. "I'm missing wrestling."

"Good to know," Irene said. "We've conducted a variety of interviews and gone over the financials. There are two issues that remain unresolved at this time. The first is Gene's extensive reimbursements, which I am still evaluating. The second is the loaning of equipment to staff and community members. This is what we'll be focusing on this evening. Katie and Gene, as you've both already been interviewed, if you could let the others answer first, that would be appreciated."

"Should I leave?" Gene asked.

"No, I'd like to have you here. I'm hoping we can get some inconsistencies straightened out. Let's start by discussing board approval of budget."

All heads turned to Gene. He shrugged.

Ava-May offered, "Annie is the treasurer. She'd know the most about that."

"Do you remember approving the budget and

looking at spending reports?" Irene pressed.

Joe responded. "Well, sure. But it isn't like we spent a lot of time on that."

"Why not?"

"Well, Gene and Phyllis prepared a monthly report. As long as the expenses were within the budgeted amounts, we'd sign off on them."

"You didn't review expenses or approve expenses with a motion?"

"No. It would have been a waste of time."

"Darrel thought we should have," Ava-May mentioned.

"Who's Darrel?" Irene asked.

Gene answered. "Darrel Berg was on the board about four years ago. He worried about fiscal responsibility."

"But you didn't worry?"

Gene met Irene's gaze. "I thought it was important, but I didn't worry about it."

"We didn't need to," Katie interrupted. "Hardly anything went over budget."

"Nothing? Ever?"

The group exchanged looks.

"A few things. Payroll is always higher than we budgeted," Joe said.

There was a general murmur of agreement.

"How would you know if something went over budget?" asked Irene. "Was it in a report?"

"I'm sure it was in the report," said Katie. "But Gene would always point out any discrepancies. I do remember a few times things went over budget, but it was never anything serious."

"You know," said Ava-May, "I don't think we did

get a financial report each month."

Irene noticed Gene's head jerk in response to this.

"I mean," she said, looking uncomfortable, "we'd get a summary. And that cute little dashboard. But the only time we got a formal report was after the audits."

"When you say dashboard, do you mean a financial summary?" Irene asked.

Ava-May nodded. "Yeah. Except it had little red, yellow, and green light symbols to show how things were going."

Katie cut in. "That's not true. We got a report that had the checks and various revenue sources."

"I think you got those," said Ava-May. "And maybe Annie. The rest of us got the dashboard."

They all pondered that.

The door swung open and an attractive woman in riding clothes strode into the room.

"Ah, Annie," said Gene. "I'm glad you're here."

"Sorry," she said to the group at large. She approached Irene and shook her hand. "Annie Cummings. I'm sorry about being late. I had a lesson go long."

"No problem," Irene said. "Maybe you can describe what kind of financial reports the board would get."

Annie swung her bag over the back of a chair and took out a binder. "I got a profit and loss ledger and the bank statements. The board would get monthly dashboard reports and quarterly P&L statements."

"What did you do if there were problems?" asked Irene.

"There were a few deviations," Annie said, "but generally things ran smoothly."

"Annie," said Katie, "is an insurance actuary. She

keeps us on the straight and narrow."

"I'm good with details," admitted Annie, "but bad with strategy. Katie moves us forward and I keep sweeping up behind the elephants." The group laughed at this long-running joke.

"So, the rest of you," Irene said, looking at the group, "were less interested in finances than you were in…?"

"Policy," Katie said firmly. "It is the board's responsibility to review policies and to make any necessary changes. We hired a good principal, and we wanted to let him do his job. He hired good teachers and staff who did their job. But we were always aware that those children were ultimately our responsibility."

Irene shifted tacts. "What is the policy governing large purchases?"

When Katie looked unsure, Annie spoke up. "The policy is to put items over five thousand dollars as a line item in the annual budget. For example, last year we needed a new tractor. And Gene felt that new computers were important for the IT lab and functional classroom areas. He also wanted to invest in some tablets that would allow the children to enter data while they were out in the field. He put those as line items in the budget, and the board approved them."

"Well," said Joe, "we didn't approve a *new* tractor. It's a new-to-us tractor."

"After items are approved," Irene said, "do you review their actual costs?"

"No," said Annie. "I review the report and if there is a problem, I let the board know."

"If there is a problem, what happens?"

"We talk about it," Annie said.

Irene stifled a groan. Boards never seemed to grasp that "talking about it" wasn't a method of documentation. "Do you approve the expenses through a vote? How do you record that you discussed the issue if there's a future problem?"

Annie looked at Katie. Katie looked nonplussed. "I never thought about that."

"Okay." Irene's eyes drifted to Gene, and she accidently met his gaze, but she quickly continued. "Let's talk about the budget itself. How did you handle changes?"

"It didn't happen often," said Ava-May. "A couple of years ago we agreed there wasn't a problem if a line-item was high as long as there was enough money in the category."

"Yeah," said Joe. "I mean, who cares if one teacher's expenses are high as long as someone else evens them out?"

"You didn't make a motion to shift items within the budget?"

They all shook their heads.

"Alright," Irene said. "Let's move on. How does Gene get board approval on various programs such as adding greenhouses or Find Your Success?"

All the board members looked to Katie.

Quickly, Irene said, "I'd like someone else to answer. Katie has already answered a version of this and so has Gene."

"Well," Joe said, looking to the others to chime in, "we have a monthly potluck. See, the board meeting is always the third Tuesday of the month. On the first Tuesday, we have a potluck at Gene's house."

"It's a simple meal," Ava-May confided. "I make

soup, Joe brings bread, Annie and Katie bring a salad or vegetable dish, and Gene does a dessert. We have dinner and talk about how things are going."

"And if something needs to be changed," Annie cut in, "it will come up there. If one of us hears a complaint from a parent, we'll talk about it. If there's a big problem, we'll problem solve. That's how these programs start. And if they are successful, they grow."

"Can anyone come to this dinner?" Irene said, making notes.

As one, they looked baffled. "Well, if someone wanted to come, we wouldn't say no."

"But it's not published anywhere?" Irene clarified.

As one, they shook their heads.

"Do you any other regular meetings off the books?" Irene asked.

They looked around.

"There's a community workday the last Saturday of every month," Joe offered. "We all try to be there. It's one of the ways we try to find out if any of the kids or parents have problems."

"But that event is publicized, correct?"

They all nodded.

Wanting to try a new angle, Irene took back the questioning. "Let's go back to the new programs. For example, the FYS funding. I've received conflicting statements about how it is funded. Can anyone fill that in for me?"

For the first time, Tyler answered. "I work on that program, specifically. I've been writing grants for it."

"It's all paid from grants?"

"No, we pay for the program benefits through the business profits. We earmark it as extracurricular activities and use it as leverage or match to other grants. We go for grants to help with the after-school investments, such as teacher overtime and bonuses which are tied to that program. To cover the rest, we have an annual fundraiser."

"What is the grant name?"

He rattled off a federal agency and grant name that Irene checked against a list.

"Let's talk specifically about Gene's reimbursements," she directed. "It's a large amount. Why have you ignored the auditor's advice about moving those to more traditional purchasing avenues?"

As one, the board members shifted in their chairs.

"We haven't ignored it," Ava-May volunteered. "But those expenses are unexpected and need to be solved in the moment."

Irene read from a list. "Since the beginning of the month, Gene has turned in reimbursement requests for ten yards of compost, several hardware store visits, a chainsaw repair, and two dozen robotics motors. The total is over twelve hundred dollars. You're only halfway through the month."

Tyler responded, "The school needed all those things."

The board members murmured in agreement.

Irene did her best to get through to them. "Yes. But why is Gene purchasing them? Why aren't they going through public procurement?"

"There isn't time," Gene snapped. "When the fields are ready, we have to move."

Irene indicated she understood the point. "Fair enough. But surely you knew compost would be necessary at some point. Why not go through channels?"

"There are two reasons," Gene said, clearly struggling for patience. "First, I can go down to the local yard and get the compost in fifteen minutes. If we 'go through channels', it takes me that long to find the correct form. Second, I prefer to support our local vendors. When we buy ten yards of compost, we probably receive half again that much as a donation."

"Those are excellent reasons. But the pattern looks suspicious."

"What pattern?" Katie interjected, shooting a wary glance at a frustrated Gene.

"The state feels purchases need to be made publicly and everyone should have a chance to bid on procurement opportunities," Irene explained. "When the public doesn't see that, it can feel like spending is in a black box. Part of our job is to make sure purchasing is as transparent as possible. By making all these private purchases, Gene runs the risk of being accused of bribes or kickbacks. We've seen cases where individuals use a cash-back credit card to generate revenue."

She paused. Looked them all in the eye individually. "That's the basis of Phyllis Dixon's accusations."

She went on. "We understand that you feel Gene isn't doing anything wrong. We're trying to get to the root of why the purchasing keeps happening this way."

Joe grunted in disgust. "We want Gene working, not filling out paperwork."

Taking a moment to regain her composure, Irene rubbed her neck. She looked at her watch. "It's almost four, and I need to be heading back to the office. Would any of you like to share your views about Phyllis Dixon's termination?"

Each board member shook their head.

"I can't say I liked her," Annie said, "but she was a competent business manager. Not a great fit with our culture, but she stayed out of the way. But the way she treated that girl, well, she can't work here. Or any other school."

"It was the last in a long line of incidents," Tyler agreed.

"She wasn't a good fit," Ava-May confided. "She interviewed well. And she had good skills. But she shouldn't have been in a school, particularly not this one."

Again, Irene looked at her watch and tried to end the interview. "We'll probably be in touch several more times over the coming weeks, but I think—"

"The big mistake was not simply letting her go after a couple of weeks," Joe summarized. "We wanted to give her a chance. The next thing we knew, her probation had expired, and she became more demanding."

****

Irene tossed her equipment into the car and settled behind the wheel. She wished Candace had been able to come because the other woman would be able to drive back. Irene's legs felt like marble pillars. She gave herself a quick assessment to ensure she wasn't having any kind of MS attack. While the fatigue was worrisome, at the moment she wasn't having any trouble controlling her movements.

She checked her phone to see the traffic status. To get home, she would have to travel west along the back roads to I-205, then south until reaching I-5. From that point, there was nearly an additional hour before she arrived back at the state motor pool lots. Her phone assured her that traffic would be miserable in all the usual places. She decided to use the back roads instead of heading straight for I-5, banking on the longer drive time would be offset by not having to sit in bumper-to-bumper traffic.

She started down the road, a winding affair that followed the river, hampering acceleration. Thirty minutes later, she took a right and headed south along the old highway 99, rather than the supposedly faster I-205 and then I-5.

She passed through suburbs bisected by the busy highway. Fast food restaurants and mini marts lined the streets, accented by a multitude of stoplights. The cars were bumper to bumper, lurching from one obstacle to the next. Once she passed through the stoplights of Canby, the road became straighter and faster, leading her toward its connection to the main highway. Once she connected to the interstate, she used the car's speaker phone to call her boss, John Fisher, at his office.

"John Fisher," he barked.

She wasn't surprised to find him there, even though it was late in the day. He was a man who habitually worked later than his staff. "It's Irene."

She visualized him glancing at his watch before asking, "Where are you?"

"Aurora. Another forty-five minutes, and I should be walking through my front door."

He grunted. "Well, what happened?"

"I'd like for you to tell me."

"Candace was out sick all day. I talked to HR and we're considering our options. But in the meantime, the case is now officially yours."

"Okay." Irene considered. "Then the answer to your question is not much happened. I have nothing to indicate the bookkeeping is out of order. Equipment is being lent out to the community, but it's coming back in good order. The reimbursements are high, but nothing about them bothers me. There are no indications that any kind of fraud or malfeasance is going on."

Irene heard John blow out a breath. "What about the attendance?"

Irene shook her head. "I've spoken to the school district, and they are willing to chalk it up to a mistake. The registrar has reviewed the numbers, Fallbrook has sent back the extra money, and everyone wants to let it go."

"Why did it happen?" John pressed.

"I don't know for sure, but I have my suspicions."

"Which are?"

"I think Phyllis Dixon went in and adjusted the reports. She shouldn't have been able to, with all the various technology and digital signatures, but she found a way. I might ask Peter to take a look at it. He's always good at figuring out a workaround."

"Yeah."

Silence fell between them.

"John," Irene began. "If this is my case now, I think it's time to write the report and call it a day."

Another grunt. "Alright. Let's connect in the morning."

"Will do," she promised.

Chapter 12

The clock on her car's dashboard reported the time as 6:19 pm when Irene turned onto her street. Door to door, the day had been twelve hours. She was so tired she almost plowed into Angie's car where it sat in her driveway. Succumbing to fatigue, Irene laid her head on the steering wheel for a minute. Her back ached and she wanted to relax. She exited the car.

She heard Angie's anguished sobbing even before she arrived at the door. The door wasn't locked, so she pushed into the entryway to find her sister on the couch, crying into Sharon's shoulder. Earlier, Irene had asked Sharon to look in on the gray dog a couple times during the day and feed him dinner. Irene guessed that Angie had waylaid Sharon during one of the visits. Sharon and Irene exchanged a look.

The dog was sitting next to the couch, offering a stuffed toy as comfort to Angie, tail wagging softly. He saw Irene and galloped toward her. Irene gave him a scratch, put down her bags, hung up her coat, and went over to Angie. Angie's eyes were puffy and red. Her makeup ran down her cheeks. Her hair lay flat in one area and puffy in another.

"He's having an affair," she wailed. "With Patricia!"

Irene searched her brain to discover if the name Patricia should mean anything significant. "Your neighbor? The one with the twins?"

"Yes!" she screamed. "Her! They are in the same class as Dave!"

"Oh god," Irene said.

Angie launched herself toward Irene. The dog spooked, running out of the room and into the kitchen.

"Okay, Angie. Let's take a—"

"Don't tell me how to breathe!" she shrieked "He's having an affair, goddamnit!"

"I hear you."

"An *affair*."

"Yes."

"With the neighbor."

"Yes."

"What am I supposed to do?" Her voice broke on the word "do".

"Angie, I'm going to take a deep breath. It was a long day. I'm tired, and my back hurts. I want to listen to you. I want to help. But I can't do that until I go pee."

Angie giggled wetly, then sank back down on the couch, sobbing again.

Irene moved to the bathroom, then changed into yoga pants and a T-shirt. She went to the kitchen and put on a pot of water to boil for tea, then crossed again to the couch to give Angie a big hug.

Sharon touched Angie's arm. "Do you want me to stay?"

Angie hiccupped. "No. You've been so nice, making sure I wasn't here alone."

"It's no problem. You've had a shock."

"More like my life is over."

"It's not over, but it's going to change. I believe in you. You're a strong woman."

This set Angie off into more crying. Deciding retreat

was the best strategy, Sharon waved at Irene as she left. The dog, who had followed Irene into the bathroom, bedroom, and kitchen, jumped up on the sofa next to her.

The three stayed like that for several minutes before the teapot whistled.

"Do you want to come up to the counter, honey? Or do you want me to bring it to you?"

"I don't want tea," she said fretfully. "I want tequila."

"Will whiskey do?" Irene asked.

"Oh, I don't know." Angie pushed up off the couch and made her way to the counter where she threw herself down onto a bar stool.

Irene stood up and began making tea, adding a generous portion of whisky to Angie's mug to make a kind of hot toddy. Angie took a sip and grimaced. "Don't you have any real liquor?"

Irene ignored that. "What happened?"

"That bitch ambushed me," she wailed.

Irene felt old. High school romance drama had confused her even when she had been a teenager. Angie had always relished melodrama. "What happened?" she repeated.

"So, I had the day off. I dropped the kids off and then ran errands. I had stopped in to get my nails done and I decided to get a pedicure, too. I was in the back chair when *she* came into the salon. She was with Cherry Lovett."

Another name Irene didn't recognize, but it was said with loathing.

"Cherry saw me, but I don't think Patricia did," Angie said. "They sat down and the techs started on their nails." For some reason, this produced another round of tears.

Irene waited, pondering how anyone could have the time to have their nails done, commit to keeping them up, and arrange it all on the same schedule with a friend.

Angie began again. "So, Cherry starts asking Patricia how it's going with her new guy. And that bitch starts going on about how Jason is such a catch and how his wife doesn't appreciate what she's got. It took me about five minutes to catch on that she was talking about my Jason." She gulped. "It never even occurred to me that she was talking about us."

Irene signaled that Angie should keep talking.

"And Cherry keeps goading her on, asking her about how the sex was and if his wife suspected. It wasn't until she started talking about that maybe he was going to have to move to Bend because his wife got a job offer that I clued in."

Tears cascading down her face, Angie tried to finish the story. "Mai, the nail tech, was starting to paint my nails when I figured it out. My brain stopped. And she kept tapping my foot, you know, like they do when they want you to move. It snapped me out of it. I threw a nail polish bottle at Cherry and ran out of the salon. My shoes are still there." She lost the battle for control and began sobbing again.

Irene rubbed her back.

Angie pushed away. "I drove home, and he was there. He was playing video games, if you can believe it. I started yelling and he started yelling back about how I was emasculating him, and he wanted to move back to Alaska. Then I saw the boys. They had been up in their rooms, and they came downstairs and were looking at us. Suddenly, I realized I was standing there in my bare feet, screaming in front of my kids, trying to get a fuckhead to admit he was wrong. I stopped, put on some boots, got in the car, and came here."

"Are the kids okay?" Irene asked.

"Jason won't leave them alone." There was a moment of silence, then Angie whispered, "I guess they are."

"Do you want me to check on them?"

"He'll know I'm here."

"I know you're both mad, but you should at least text him and make sure he can stay there."

"Why? They are his children. He has just as much responsibility as I do."

"Because they are children and you are their parent," Irene said gently.

"I can't interact with him. Will you call?"

"Okay." Irene got up and went to the phone in the kitchen. A few minutes later, she returned to the living room. "He says there is no problem tonight. He says his shift starts at noon tomorrow and the babysitter is already lined up."

Angie hung her head.

"He also said he's going to give his notice at the dealership tomorrow."

She jerked, fired up again. "Like I give a fuck."

"That's fine. But he thought you should know."

"Asshole. So, he's going to chuck it all and leave me to pick up for him. Again."

Irene left that alone "Have you eaten?"

Angie shook her head.

"Do you want me to make you something? Grilled cheese?"

She smiled. "With a smiley face?"

"Is there any other kind?"

Irene started to prepare the sandwiches.

"You know the other night, when I brought over the kids?"

"I remember."

"He left his phone at the house. He told me it was because he didn't want to drop it when he was skiing. But that wasn't why. He was with her and didn't want me to use the tracker program to follow him."

Surprised, Irene turned to look at Angie. "Would you do that?"

"Oh yeah."

"Angie, it's none of my business, but has Jason had other affairs?"

A few moments of silence passed. "I haven't been able to prove it."

She set the first sandwich on Angie's plate. "I'm so sorry."

Listlessly Angie cut the sandwich into triangles and offered one to Irene. Irene took it with a smile before dropping the next sandwich onto the grill.

"When he came home from 'skiing', he got the messages I had left on his phone. I told him the boys were with you because I couldn't find a sitter."

"He showed up here less than two hours after you dropped them off."

In the middle of a bite, Angie made a noise. "I was at the hospital sorting through that worker's paperwork until past midnight. Jason didn't call to let me know he was back or that he had picked up the boys. If I hadn't called him one last time before heading down, I wouldn't have known that."

Irene thought that was particularly awful but

decided against saying anything.

They finished their dinner and lingered for a few moments. "I'm so sorry, Angie."

Angie closed her eyes. "You never think it will turn out this way."

The sisters settled on the couch to watch a favorite movie, the gray dog curling up next to Irene for petting. She was pleased he had behaved so well with Angie.

Irene texted her boss that she would be an hour late in the morning, then checked her messages. There was a hysterical rant from Angie, who had called as she was driving to Irene's house.

The second message was from Gary, "*Hey, Irene, this is Gary. I wanted to touch base with you about going to the show this weekend. Give me a call.*"

Irene smiled.

Chapter 13

The next day, Irene was exhausted. She hadn't slept well, interrupted twice by the sounds of Angie's phone ringing and her subsequent arguments with Jason. In the morning, Irene found a note that Angie had decided to go back home while the children were at school and face Jason before he left for work.

Irene called John to let him know she'd be late but still arrived before the weekly meeting. She filled her large coffee cup and took a seat in the large conference room. Others filed into the room. As usual, Candace took the seat next to Irene, and they exchanged hellos. Irene noted the other woman looked pale and tired and immediately felt bad for her unkind thoughts of the day before. Mostly.

John glanced at his watch and urged, "Let's get going, people."

Following the previously established ritual, the staff briefed their co-workers on investigations and reports.

Candace's turn came. "Well, I've been out with the flu most of the week. I'm afraid I don't have progress to report. I know Irene conducted interviews at Fallbrook yesterday."

Irene took out her notes. "Yes. While I have a few more things to check, I'm going to focus on drafting a report and marking this case closed."

Candace's eyes widened. "What about Phyllis

Dixon?"

John interrupted Irene's possible answer. "Let's talk about that off-line."

Looking confused, Candace glanced down at her notes, ceding the point.

Irene talked about a couple other cases on her plate before giving the floor back to John.

"My final item is some upcoming staffing adjustments," he stated.

All eyes focused on him.

"As most, if not all, of you have told me," John began wryly, "the department's workload is heavy. Many of you have expressed difficulty in managing your workload. With this in mind, I have decided to use some of our staff savings to open a limited duration senior investigator position, listing it as an underfill opportunity."

Staff looked at each other, shifting in agitation.

"In practical terms, I think this will mean we have to hire for a replacement junior investigator," John went on. "Both positions will be posted at the same time to allow us to interview candidates and fill positions more quickly."

"Wait—"

"Does this mean—"

"What about—"

John waved his hand to tamp down the noise and confusion. "I'll be putting out a memo this afternoon that will answer your questions." He closed his laptop. "Alright, let's get going. Candace and Irene, please stay here for a few minutes."

One the room had cleared of most staffers, John got up and reseated himself next to Candace with a view of

Irene. "Candace, I gave the Fallbrook report to Irene to finish. You have other things on your plate, and we need to get this out the door."

Irene might have expected Candace to be hurt—she would have been—but the other woman began to cry, startling her and John.

"I just can't seem to get on top of anything these days," she said, continuing to sob. "I'm working as hard as I can, but the cases keep piling up. Troy has to take care of all the kid stuff, because I'm either working or commuting."

Irene and John exchanged a confused look over the top of Candace's head.

"Candace, we can talk—" John began.

"Are you going to do something about Phyllis?" Candace asked angrily, changing topics. "I have to know that people like her, people who are deliberately making things even more awful, are being punished."

Irene remained silent, unsure what to say.

"Why can't we do something about her?" Candace wailed. "She's clearly out of bounds. Schools are there to teach and protect, not be swept up into someone's political agenda. She broke the terms of her employment contract multiple times over."

Irene waited.

"I know what you're thinking. We can't charge her with anything. It's not our department, not our authority. But why can't we turn the story over the newspapers or something?"

"For what purpose?"

"So, everyone can see what a terrible person she is."

"To what purpose?" Irene repeated.

Candace lapsed into silence.

Irene chose her words with caution. "I've thought about it. She'd get some hate mail. Maybe someone would yell at her. She might even lose a job or have to move. But in the end, that starts to feel like we're putting more of what we don't want out into the world."

"So, we ignore it and let her go," Candace summarized.

Irene thought about what to say next. "We can't solve every problem."

Silence built again. Candace took another tissue.

John interrupted the silence. "Why are you pushing this so hard?"

Candace was silent for so long, Irene thought she might not reply. Voice husky from tears, Candace eventually murmured, "Nothing's going right."

"I agree. It's unfair to leave her in the clear," Irene responded. "There might be another option."

"No—" John started.

"What?" Candace blurted.

Neither continued, so Irene continued. "In the past, we've usually focused on fraud and embezzlement. You and I agree that there are some questionable practices, but no evidence of wrongdoing."

"Yeah."

"That means that we've taken this as far as we can. The wrongful termination is the other big issue, but that's not ours. I don't see it going anywhere." Irene summarized.

John nodded. "True."

"But we haven't pursued the forgery charges," Irene pointed out.

Both Candace and John appeared startled.

John said, "We've prosecuted them before."

Irene dipped her chin. "But usually only if there is overwhelming proof and as an addition to other counts. Gene and Chick have worked the numbers out with the school district, but no one has looked into how the problem happened. I think I can prove how the attendance reports were changed and that Phyllis did it. We can use that to get her to back down."

Candace blotted her eyes with a tissue. "You think you can do that?"

"If I can prove it, it's forgery. Even if we can't, it's something to hit her with."

Candace thought about it. "It's weak. She's a nasty one."

Irene agreed. "Yes. And she has a grudge. I think she'll keep coming after Gene until she stirs up something. With this, we have something to make her back down." She paused. "I'm not sure we couldn't get the same results by pursuing charges of assault and harassment on that student, but this way, the child doesn't have to testify."

Candace tapped her fingers on the desk. "Yeah. That would be good."

John stepped in. "As I said, I'm turning this over to Irene to finish. I'd like to schedule a time for us to meet to talk about the other issues you identified. Candace, it sounds like you're having a difficult time, and I'd like to find a way to help."

Candace agreed. "Yeah. I'm not doing anyone any good." She paused. "But I still hate to let her off the hook."

"It might be more satisfying to charge her, but she's lost her job and can't do any more damage to the school. They need to move on."

Candace turned to John. "Can you give me fifteen minutes before meeting?"

He nodded, and she left the room. He turned to Irene. "I'm not sure we should use our resources to pursue these forgery charges. But I'm not the lead investigator on this case. You are."

\*\*\*\*

Irene spent the rest of the day triaging her email and paperwork. She mentally resigned herself to devoting time to catch up over the weekend. She was continually interrupted by people stopping to chat about Candace. After their meeting, John had sent out an all-staff memo that Candace was taking the rest of the day off. But as everyone had seen the morning meeting, they wanted to see if Irene knew anything else.

Irene's desk phone rang. She'd turned off her mobile phone to avoid Angie and hoped her sister hadn't decided to start calling her at work.

"Good afternoon, this is Irene Lisner. How can I help you?"

"He's cheating on her!" The shrill announcement came from Jennifer. Her mother had obviously been frustrated by her disabled mobile phone.

Irene flinched away from the phone and said calmly, "I know. She was at my house last night. She stayed with me."

"He's cheating. On her."

Irene remained silent.

"Are you still there?"

"Yes, I'm here, Jennifer."

"That two-timing, wanna-be, loser is cheating on *her*."

"Evidently."

"Did you know?"

"No."

"Nothing?"

"Nothing. I knew they were going through a rough patch because of this job offer."

"What job offer?"

Jennifer's loud voice carried, and she felt eyes on her to judge her side of the conversation. Trying to keep her voice low, Irene responded, "I'm sorry. I thought you knew. Angie got a promotion offer to manage the Lexus dealership in Bend. Jason was not excited about it. "

"And you knew this?"

"He stopped by one morning to vent."

"He stopped by? Your house?"

"I was surprised, too."

"Why didn't you tell me?"

"You and Angie talk more regularly than we do. I thought you knew or would know before I could tell you. And I'm not even sure it's something I should tell you. It's her decision."

"Oh my gosh. Do you think she'll take it?"

"I don't know."

"Right. But can you believe that *he's* cheating on *her*?"

"Jennifer, I'm at work. I don't want to have this conversation here. Did you need something specific?"

"I wanted to make sure you knew," Jennifer said sulkily.

"I do know. Have you talked to Angie today?"

"No, last night."

Irene smirked. It wasn't like Jennifer had been desperate to share the news.

"I know you go to bed early," Jennifer said

defensively. "And I had to show a house early this morning."

"It's fine. I hoped you had heard from her today. She went back home this morning and said she'd have it out with Jason."

"She hasn't called today."

Irene visualized Jennifer flipping through her phone, checking for missed calls. "It's fine," Irene reassured her. "I'm sure she'll tell us when she wants us to know."

"I guess," Jennifer agreed, but without enthusiasm.

Irene sensed an opportunity. "I've got to go now."

"Okay."

Irene got up to stretch. Her hips and legs were sore. She'd done too much this past weekend and had skipped her yoga class in order to give the dog extra exercise. As she walked down the hall, she realized her legs weren't simply sore, they were numb. She returned to her desk and pulled up her calendar to add reminders. She looked at the various notations and wondered how she could fit a new dog into it all.

She returned to the report, but her mind wasn't on the task. She kept turning over the Fallbrook School case. Something was nagging her.

\*\*\*\*

Irene returned home that evening and considered turning off her phone and heading straight to bed. She hadn't heard from Angie and was waiting for the other shoe to drop. The dog greeted her with a series of energetic twirls. He needed to blow off steam.

She changed into walking gear, leashed the dog, and picked up a flashlight. It was February, so the days were getting longer, but it was still dark in the evenings. It was drizzling lightly, but the gray dog didn't mind. She pulled up the hood on her jacket and set off.

After only a week, the dog was so much better on the leash. Confidence had never been an issue, but the first few days had been about keeping him on the sidewalk. Now he jogged down the street, sniffing at each fascinating smell. Irene watched him carefully. She still didn't trust him not to dart into the street or after a cat hiding in the bushes.

The increased daily walks had taken a toll. She was out of practice caring for a young, energetic dog. Percy had been old and content to ramble along. During the last year of his life, he hadn't been able to go on any kind of extended hiking. Percy had enjoyed his walks but had been as happy going around the block as to the park. She hadn't realized how much not walking daily had affected her. She wasn't used to walking as an endurance sport.

Saturday, Irene and Sharon went to Minto Brown Park and walked more than four miles of trails. On Sunday, Irene had taken the dog out to hike E.E. Wilson Wildlife Area, racking up even more miles. At the time, she'd noticed a variety of twinges and numbness but put it down to being out of shape.

This evening, however, everything was worse. She turned around earlier than planned, hoping to make it back to the house in one piece. Her hip was numb. Her shoulders and neck ached and each time the dog pulled on the leash, it felt worse. Her limbs felt heavy. When she stumbled for the third time, Irene realized it wasn't fatigue. She was having an MS attack.

She and the dog were near Englewood Park. Irene found a bench and sat. After the dog jumped up on the bench to keep her company, Irene got out her phone.

"Hey, Sharon. I'm taking the dog for a walk, and I'm stuck in Englewood Park. Can you come get me? Yes, I'm having a problem. Thanks."

She hung up and scratched the dog's ears while they waited. When she saw Sharon's car, she pushed herself off the bench and made her way to the car. When the dog saw Sharon, he lunged forward, which threw Irene off balance. She stumbled, fell, and dropped the leash.

Fortunately, Sharon caught Max. She stashed him in her car, then came back to help Irene back onto her feet. "How long has it been like this?" she asked gently.

"It's worse today. I didn't get enough sleep last night, and I overdid it on the weekend."

"Okay. Let's get you home. Does Max still need some exercise?"

"No. He did his business. I was trying to get some of his energy out."

"Okay."

Sharon got Irene and the dog home in minutes, then stashed Irene in a chair with a cup of tea. She took the dog outside to see if he would chase a ball. Foolish question. Ten minutes later, the dog pranced into the room, eyes gleaming, the ball in his mouth. He dropped it at her feet and backed up a few paces, clearly hoping she would play. Sharon coaxed the dog to exchange the ball for a cookie. He made the trade, then jumped up on the couch to enjoy his snack.

Sharon sat on the sofa. "Do you want to talk about it?"

Irene looked out the window at the dark street, the same scene she had been watching for the last ten minutes. "I don't know."

Silence settled between them. After a minute,

Sharon asked, "How's Angie?"

Irene shrugged. "She hasn't called me yet. She left this morning to 'have it out' with Jason. And I haven't heard anything since."

"Do you think that's good or bad?"

"I have no idea. Part of me hopes they straightened things out and are spending some time making up. Part of me thinks that this is the calm before the storm."

"Did she say she would call today?"

"Yeah," Irene said wearily. "She said she'd let me know how it went."

"Okay." Sharon looked out at the night scene. They sat in silence together for a few minutes.

"I really like this dog," Irene said. "But I don't think I can keep him."

"Why not?"

"Look at me. I've had him a week and I'm falling apart." With those few words, her voice broke.

Sharon sat calmly for a few minutes, waiting for her to go on.

"He's everything I'd look for in a performance dog. He's smart. He's trainable. He loves attention, toys, and treats." Irene took a shaky breath. "But I think he's more than I can handle."

"You're probably right," Sharon said, shocking Irene. "He's more than you can handle *alone.* Irene, one of the things I admire about you is that you are independent. But this isn't something you have to do alone. Hire a dog walker. Enroll him in doggie day care. Ask me to be a backup handler if you want. But you, personally, don't have to do every damn thing."

Irene looked at her. "What's the point of having a dog if I can't do stuff with him? I mean, if it's all going to be short walks, maybe it's better to get an old dog."

"That's always an option, and you and I know that there are wonderful old dogs out there. But I can tell how much you like this dog. And he likes you. I agree, he's a great performance prospect. You do not have to make him into a competition dog all by yourself."

Irene shook my head. "I don't know, Sharon."

"Why? No, seriously, why? Because it's not all you?"

Irene looked away, shaking her head again.

"Okay. Think about it," Sharon soothed. "You're tired tonight. It's been a bad day. Don't make any decisions. I'll come over in the morning to walk the dog."

"You don't have to—"

"I'll be walking Mule anyway. What's one more? Have an extra cup of coffee and go to work. I'll take care of it."

"Thank you," Irene said. "And thank you for coming to get me. And for paying—"

"Don't," Sharon interrupted. "Irene, I love you, honey. This is what friends do. It's not payback."

Irene stood up and gave Sharon a hug. "Thank you, anyway."

****

Angie called just as Irene was settling the dog in his kennel and settling down to read for a few minutes. Bracing herself, Irene picked up the phone. "Hey, Angie."

"Hey." The word was said without enthusiasm.

"How'd it go?" Irene asked gently.

"We've decided to separate. I accepted the job in Bend. The boys and I will move by the end of next month. Jason says he's going to move back to Alaska and turned in his notice today."

Irene was silent for a moment. "Wow."

"Wow," Angie repeated.

"Is there anything I can do to help?" Irene asked, wondering what she'd do if Angie took her up on her offer.

There was a moment of silence. "Not right now, I think. The company will move me, so it isn't something I'll need to do on my own. I'll try to schedule a packing party and if you can help with that, I'd appreciate it." She paused, then continued. "We told the boys tonight. That's why I'm calling so late. They're upset, particularly Dave. If you could call them tomorrow and maybe take them out for a day soon, I think that would help."

"Okay," Irene said.

"Irene—" Her voice broke, and she took a deep breath. "Irene, I didn't want this."

"I know, honey."

"I begged him to stay." Irene blinked in surprise but said nothing. "I told him we could do counseling. I even told him"—she sobbed—"that we'd come to Alaska. And he said no. He said he was tired of me and the suburbs and this whole life. I asked him how he could be tired of the boys and he said that he still loved them, but he couldn't waste his life stuck as a house husband."

"Oh, honey."

"How could he think that?"

"He's upset. He's confused. When things calm down, he'll probably be sorry he said that."

"I love him."

"I know, sweetie."

"I don't understand how we got here."
"I know."

Chapter 14

Thursday morning, the office was filled with hardworking state employees. Irene found it fascinating that any kind of shake up, such as adding a new senior investigator, would inspire a fierce work ethic.

John had worked a miracle and got the new positions posted. Peter had already applied for the senior investigator position, and one of the office staffers had applied for the junior investigator position. The interviews were scheduled for early next week, another minor miracle.

To give herself a break, Irene had made the rare concession of driving to work. She felt unusually fragile and hoped the concession would provide her some relief.

Coffee in hand, she stepped into a small conference room for her session with Peter. She set down her notes and drew out her laptop, intending to plug it into the projection system. Before she could start, Peter appeared and took care of the task.

"I could have done that," she protested.

Peter waved her off, "Drink your coffee. Or tell me what's up."

"I need your help to figure something out." She explained her suspicions about the discrepancy between the prepared reports and what was actually sent to the education district.

"Well, it shouldn't be too hard," Peter mused. "All

we have to do is check the meta data."

Irene felt her eyes cross. "Peter, if this is going to get technical, I'll leave, and you can tell me what you find."

He laughed and shook his head. "It's not. Do you have the report as the registrar prepared it?"

Irene pointed to the projection of her laptop on the screen.

"Right click the document," he directed, "then go to Properties and open it up."

Irene followed his instructions.

"Huh. Well, that's disappointing," Peter commented.

Irene's impatience mounted. "What?"

"Disappointing because you took this document from the school's server and copied it to your own computer, the program has stripped out the generative data."

"What?"

Peter pointed to the screen. "See how it says some properties have been blocked for security reasons?"

"Yeah."

"The state's security checked it and wiped it."

"So, we can't find out?"

Peter shrugged. "Not on this computer. If we went to the site, we could check their documents. The information would almost definitely be saved."

Irene pursed her lips. "Could it be done over video conference? I don't have time to drive down there again."

"That might work," Peter agreed.

"Do you think this properties thing would be enough to show we've got a good case?

Peter studied the projection screen. "I'm not sure. The information here is a good first step. Creation and modification dates prove things have been changed. Can you open the documents and put them side by side on the screen?"

Irene worked on the request, slowly adjusting the images.

"Oh, let me do it," Peter said, coming across the room.

She moved so he could drive the computer. Within moments the two documents were side-by-side on the screen. "You see that?" Peter pointed.

She didn't.

He got up. "You see how the fonts are different in this area?"

Now that he had pointed it out, she could clearly see the document prepared by Chick was completely in a serif font. But in the document submitted by Phyllis, the central enrollment numbers were in a sans serif font.

"My guess is that she put the document in a simple imaging program and overlaid the original numbers with her own."

Irene thought about that for a moment. "Anything else?"

Peter moved the cursor to a menu item and asked the PDF program to compare the documents. "The report from Chick shows as having authentic signatures. The other one doesn't show as having any signatures, even though we can see them. That leads me to believe that the document from Phyllis is based in an imaging software, not a word-based form."

Confused, Irene said, "I thought digital signature were supposed to be secure. I mean, if they aren't, why is there such a fuss around using them?" Months before, there had been a series of tedious memos from the state's central office about procedures to set up and use digital signatures.

Peter pointed at one side of the screen. "They are secure. But only if someone actually verifies them. With laser printers and hi-res imaging, it's easy to create a fake that passes at a glance."

Irene struggled with a feeling of intense insecurity. "Thanks, Peter. I think this will be enough, but if I need more, I know where to come."

\*\*\*\*

Irene arranged to meet with former board member, Darrel Berg, Friday morning before final meetings with Katie Maldonado and Gene Schuster. She had debated trying to conduct these final meetings via video but admitted that would be less effective and resigned herself to another drive. Next, she called her contact at the education department for an in-depth conversation about the school's agricultural programs and special services.

Irene laid out the case for the education representative. They discussed some of the more problematic information, but they agreed that the school's programs were within statutory authority. Irene explained her theory on the attendance reports and her counterpart agreed with her assessment of the situation. Finally, they covered the small, for-profit businesses attached to the school, but neither could find any evidence of incorrect accounting. Irene laid out her proposed solution to the inquiry and the school expert agreed with it.

Irene had barely signed off from the conference call when the room's phone buzzed. Uncertainly, she picked it up.

"Irene, Phyllis Dixon is waiting in the lobby for you. She's been waiting for a half hour." Though Mishel was whispering, Irene recognized her voice.

"We didn't have an appointment," she pointed out.

"I know. But she won't leave."

Irene rubbed her forehead. "Alright. Tell her I'll be out in five minutes."

Quickly, she removed her equipment from the conference room, then visited the bathroom. She picked up a fresh cup of coffee before heading back to the front to meet with Phyllis Dixon.

And found Candace Fernandez lurking at reception.

"Did you see her?" Candace whispered.

Irene felt a surge of bitterness. Candace could ignore Phyllis, but Irene still had to deal with her. Irene reminded herself that her attitude was the only thing she could control. "Yeah. I'll take her to the conference room and find out what she wants."

Moving past Candace, Irene greeted the former business manager. "Good morning, Phyllis. I'm sorry to make you wait, but we didn't have an appointment."

Her face flushed with anger and frustration, Phyllis snapped, "I demand to know why you are allowing that school to smear my good name."

Irene blinked. "I'm afraid you have me at a disadvantage. I don't know what you are talking about."

Phyllis snorted in disgust.

"Why don't you come into the conference room? Then you can fill me in."

Phyllis followed Irene like rain following a cloud.

"Would you like some coffee?" Irene asked.

"No, thank you."

After Phyllis took a seat, Irene lowered herself into the uncomfortable conference room chairs. "Okay. What's going on?"

Phyllis scowled. "Yesterday, as I'm sure you're aware, I had a meeting with the state's investigator about my wrongful termination suit. He asked me about what happened, then asked me a bunch of questions about how I interacted with the board and the students." She huffed out an angry breath. "He told me Katie Maldonado said I was a bad hire, and they should have let me go earlier."

Irene didn't react for a few moments. She remembered Katie telling her then had made a mistake in hiring Phyllis "I'm afraid I'm still not understanding the problem."

"I have never in my life received anything but a glowing job review," Phyllis wailed. "Why are they being allowed to change that? They are trashing my reputation."

"I have very little power over other peoples' reputations or what others say about them," Irene pointed out. "People believe what they want."

"So, you're taking their side."

"I'm taking the side of the State of Oregon, which doesn't have a dog in this particular fight."

Phyllis glared. "All I'm trying to do is report him for wasting money and circumventing the rules. And I'm the one on trial."

Irene gazed at her for a long moment, sizing up the situation. "Phyllis, let me be frank. You've made some serious allegations about wrongdoing in the Fallbrook School. The board, the district, the county, and the state are taking you seriously. We're investigating. But you can't expect to throw mud and not get some on yourself."

"I didn't do anything wrong."

"We haven't said you have."

Phyllis continued her glare.

Irene sipped her coffee. After a moment, she broke the silence. "There are questions that we still need to ask. Do you mind if we do that now?"

Phyllis looked out the window. "Fine. Ask your questions."

"Okay." Irene reviewed her notes. "Tell me what financial information the Fallbrook board received at each board meeting."

Phyllis scowled. "It varied. There was a general board packet that contained dashboards and overviews. Katie and Annie would get a more detailed report that included investments, budgets, account payable, and the check register with any handwritten checks highlighted."

"Why did they get a different budget report?"

"Katie and Annie requested a report that showed what was spent in the budget and the remaining balance of the budget. The others received a simplified version."

"What was your role in the board meetings?"

"I did the prep work. Katie and Annie would ask me to do various reports. I'd get the minutes typed up—"

"Who took the minutes?" Irene interrupted.

"The school secretary, Ms. Sutton, would stay and take the notes. Then I'd type them, store them, and get them on the internet to meet records requirements."

"Okay. What did you do during the meetings?"

"It was Gene's show. He'd go over all the expenses and the board would nod and move on."

Irene asked a few more questions, receiving short, sulky answers. Letting off steam about the interview had turned Phyllis snarky and unresponsive. That was fine with Irene. She had tied up almost all the loose ends and her questions were largely unnecessary.

After Phyllis left, Candace walked with Irene to her office. "Mishel said she was waiting more than a half hour. She tried to get her to sit down and have a drink, but she kept pacing and asking when you'd arrive."

Irene rolled her head to stretch her neck. "At least it spared me from making another appointment with her."

"What are you going to do?" asked Candace.

Irene shrugged. "I don't think she intended to scam anyone. I think she got impatient."

Candace looked skeptical. "That's a pretty benign way to look at it."

"A benign tumor is still a form of cancer."

****

At her desk, Irene worked on finishing the first draft of the Fallbrook report. She kept an eye on her inbox, which filled at an alarming rate. During lunch, she checked her personal email with her phone. There was an email from Marion County Dog Control.

*Irene,*

*We have a potential adopter for Max. The information is attached.*

*Give him a call and set up a time and place to meet so he gets acquainted with Max.*

*Let me know if you have any questions.*

*Ashley*

Irene's heart sank. She took a drink from the water bottle on her desk. She reminded herself that keeping the dog wasn't a real option. This was probably a sign that he was ready to move on.

When Irene called the number of the adopter, a hearty voice answered, "Neal Slater."

"Hello, Mr. Slater. My name is Irene and I'm a volunteer with Marion County Animal Control. I understand you are interested in meeting my current foster, Max?"

"Yes. I'd love to meet him. How does it work?"

"Well," Irene said, "this is my first time, too. But the county told me that we could meet at the shelter, if that works for you. I understand it's open until six in the evening."

"Can't do it tonight. What about Friday night? Around four?"

"Unfortunately, I don't think that would be a good time. He has his neuter appointment that day and he'll be woozy. What about Saturday morning? Around eleven?"

"I can do that. What can you tell me about him?" Neal asked.

Irene described their progress, emphasizing that this was a smart, young dog who needed exercise and wasn't fully housetrained.

Neal responded with, "Yeah, yeah." Or, "I had a dog like that." When she got to the part about house training, he sounded hesitant. "You mean, he's not potty trained?"

"Well, he's working on it. I'm being careful not to let him have a mistake in the house. I think you should spend a few months watching him to be sure he's got the idea, especially in a new environment."

"I thought he'd be potty trained," Neal said.

Irene looked at the phone. She returned it to her ear and said, "Like I said, he'll need some consistent effort on that."

"I don't know if my wife will like that," he muttered.

Irene felt her brows knit. "She should come along and meet him too. After all, he'll be a part of the family."

She heard a grunt at the other end. "She's in a wheelchair," Neal admitted.

Irene's misgivings increased. "Will she be able to… ah… handle such an energetic dog?"

"Oh, it won't be a problem. We had a collie mix for years. Just loved to sit in your lap, but if the doorbell rang, she was there like a shot."

"How long did you have her?"

"Twelve years. She passed last month, and our little poodle needs a friend. I looked at this one's picture on the site and he's a dead ringer for a dog I had when I was a kid. He was a real good dog. Helped us out on the farm, never let us kids get into trouble."

Irene suppressed a groan. Nostalgia was nice, but an unrealistic replacement for exercise and training. "I'm sure Max would love a farm."

"Oh, we don't have a farm. We live in one of those retirement communities. It's all townhouses. But it's next to some short trails, so he'll like that."

"Right. Okay, well, I'll see you on Saturday then."

"Sure. See you there."

After he hung up, Irene emailed Ashley.

*Ashley,*

*I called Mr. Slater. Are you sure this is a good fit? He doesn't seem to realize how young and energetic Max is. He expressed concern about house training. There is another small dog in the household. His wife is in a wheelchair. It doesn't sound like a good spot for Max.*

*Irene*

A few minutes later, her phone beeped, and she looked down to see the new email icon. She clicked it.

*He was the first adopter to put in an application. He met all the requirements. But after they meet, if you think it's a bad fit, I can talk to him. But these things usually have a way of working out. Don't worry.*

*Unless you want to keep him?*

*Ashley*

Irene didn't reply.

Chapter 15

Friday morning, Irene dropped the dog off at Willamette Humane Society for his neuter appointment. He stopped halfway down the hall, looked back at her, and whined piteously. She couldn't have felt worse if he'd been dragged down the hall.

Her busy day would keep her mind off the dog. She had the final set of meetings for Fallbrook. Irene had set up her first meeting at a coffee place near the highway that would take her to the town. Irene had no trouble picking out Darrel Berg because they had exchanged descriptions when arranging the appointment. He was a tall, good-looking man in his seventies, trim and fit and wore clothes that were casual but spoke of exclusivity. Irene noticed he arrived in an expensive sedan. She waved to him. and they shook hands. After ordering their coffee drinks, they sat down at a small table in the corner.

Irene hoped Darrel could shed light on his fiscal concerns during his time on the Fallbrook board. Katie Maldonado had mentioned him as an advocate of responsible stewardship for the school's money. Irene was interested in his perspective. "Thank you for meeting me, Mr. Berg."

"Call me Darrel," he urged.

"Thank you," she acknowledged. "As I said on the phone, I want to chat with you about your time on the board of Fallbrook School District."

"What have they gotten themselves into?" he asked, exasperation floating across his face.

"Why would you think they had gotten into something?" Irene countered.

"It was only a matter of time," Darrel said. "I've never seen a group so uninterested in finances."

Irene signaled her understanding. "Getting a board who understands that sort of thing can be tricky."

He sipped his drink, then leaned forward. "Irene, I volunteered for that board because my son asked me to. My granddaughter had gone through some things that… well… no one should go through. She loves that school and is finally starting to heal. Chris asked me to sit on the board because he was concerned that Schuster or one of those other hippies would get the school involved in some crazy scheme. He would have done it himself, but he doesn't have the time."

Irene nodded. "And did they have crazy schemes?"

He shook his head. "No. Their ideas were sound. They paid attention to the programs. But trying to get them to talk about money was a lost cause."

"What kinds of things did you want to talk about?" she asked.

"I wanted to find out how money was used. When I tried to get information on individual programs, Gene would point out that the overall budget was intact. As long as we weren't overspending, no one was interested in any more detail. I can't count the number of times I asked for a report listing the entire individual grant programs and their accompanying spending. Finally, I told Katie that I wanted to help, but that I couldn't put my name to something so vague. It was only a matter of time before something or someone went wrong and the school would end up in the papers."

"Did you ever discuss your concerns with Gene?" Irene asked.

"I did. He was pleasant about it, but it was like he didn't trust me to help. He pulled up reports and we talked about them, but when I suggested some ways I could help, he said thanks but no thanks."

"How did you offer to help?"

"At the time, they were ramping up for the restoration plant program. I suggested that I could call one of my contacts at the Bonneville Environmental Foundation and ask if there was some way the school could get on their list of contractors."

"What did he say?"

"'Thank you, but we're as busy as we can handle.' I suggested I could help with some grant writing. He told me they weren't applying for grants at the moment. I also suggested that we could bring some of my business contacts in to mentor some of the kids who were interested in the business side. Schuster was uninterested."

"Why do you think that was?"

"I don't know. Maybe he's burned out from people who offer to help but never follow through. I made sure to follow up a couple of times, but it didn't make a difference."

Irene made a note. "Did you feel like the problem was him? Staff? Board members?"

Darrel thought about the question for a moment. "I'm not sure. They were more interested in creating new programs than making sure the financial foundation was solid. Toward the end of my tenor, I spent some time cobbling together reports and other information. I realized that most of the discretionary money was going to these 'new programs' rather than straight education."

"I assume you haven't heard about the difficulties facing the school now?"

He shook his head.

"Gene fired the business manager who is filing suit for wrongful termination. In turn, she had made a variety of accusations about the board not following proper financial protocols. Do you have any thoughts about that?"

"This is Phyllis Dixon, right?"

Irene agreed.

"I never worked with her while I was on the board, but I met her a couple of times when I visited the school. I'm not surprised she's creating a fuss. She's that type. But if I'm following what you are saying, I'd be surprised if her accusations of improper finances were true. My complaint with the board and Schuster is that they weren't focusing on the basics of financial management and investing. They were coasting along, letting the business manager deal with it."

Irene looked at her notes. "At the time, that was a different financial manager?"

He dipped his head in agreement. "Maggie. She was good. A real jewel. I was disappointed when she retired." He shook his head. "Without her, I'm surprised it took this long to have problems."

Irene made a note. "Did you have any other concerns about the school?"

"Like what?"

Irene shrugged. "Teachers, students, curriculum, whatever."

Darrel shook his head. "No. It was remarkably quiet.

Schuster ran a tight ship. The teachers were dedicated. I was surprised he didn't get more pushback about discipline from the parents, but he handled it."

"What does that mean?"

Darrel shrugged. "Kids who misbehaved got detention, which meant extra hours in the fields and any other unpleasant task Gene could find. He's a big believer in the expression, 'a tired kid is a good kid'."

Irene smiled. "I've only heard that with dogs."

"Same principle."

****

At Fallbrook, Irene saw children around the grounds. Some of the younger children were at recess, but a group of kindergarteners were in a small plot of land that had barrels. Irene observed a teacher open the top of one and the children "ewwwwed" when she lifted out a handful of dirt with worms wriggling. Older children were working around the gardens and greenhouses.

A set of students measured soil into test tubes under a teacher's watchful eye while another set of children worked with small, colored strips in a different set of test tubes. Soil PH testing, Irene guessed, noting a large chart behind the group filled with writing. Irene saw how the workings of the various enterprises could be tied into lessons and benefit students.

It was impossible to view these programs and hear people talk about the good they had done and not want the school to succeed. Irene grieved for the damage accusations and misjudgments caused.

Irene met Katie Maldonado in the front office, and they moved to a small conference room. "Thank you for meeting with me again, Katie," Irene began.

She waved her hand. "*De nada*. I'd like to get this thing over with. Ask what you need to."

"I'll give you an update, then I need to ask you a few questions." Irene began her recap. "As you know, my office is not involved in the lawsuit about unlawful termination. That's a civil matter, and it will be up to the board if you want to counter her allegations or move to some other resolution."

Katie frowned but remained silent.

"We have reviewed the school's financials. While we cannot find any wrongdoing, my report will contain strong wording about our belief there is a significant gap in board oversight."

When Katie sputtered, Irene held up her hand. "The board approved a budget and reviews spending, which is what they should do. But when we dig deeper, it becomes obvious that Gene is the one responsible for most, if not all, of the day-to-day budgetary decisions."

"Of course," said Katie. "That's what we hired him to do. And we're letting him do it."

Irene inclined her head. "That's one interpretation, and it's a good one. The problem is that many decisions and actions are never making it to a review by the board. The biggest example of this is the amount of Gene's reimbursements. He has paid out and been reimbursed more than fifty-five thousand over the last five years. Most of the purchases were small items that might have been purchased through more traditional channels."

Katie looked confused.

Irene explained. "A typical example would be Gene going to get office supplies after work instead of using the state contract. Not only would the school have saved a couple dollars on price, but the office supply store would also have delivered the items the next day for free."

"I thought we had a contract for office supplies," Katie said, looking confused.

Irene smiled. "You do. But the perception has become that it's too time-consuming to use it. It's impossible to say how you got to this stage, but the board is turning a blind eye by not spending more time examining expenses and contracts and leaving Gene to pick up the slack."

Katie thought about this for a few moments. "And you'll be putting this in your report?"

"Yes. I will be making some recommendations regarding strengthening separation of duties and moving some responsibilities away from Gene. That's not a reflection on Gene. At every opportunity, he has impressed me as a talented, hard-working educator. This is a reflection that the board needs to let him be an educator and take a more active role in guidance."

Katie inclined her head reluctantly.

"Okay," Irene said, looking down at her notes. "The last issue is a program audit. I spoke to my contact at the education department. She had a couple of concerns which I will include in my report. On the enterprise programs—"

"What are enterprise programs?" Katie asked.

"An enterprise program refers to school activities that make money."

Katie dipped her head in understanding.

"The initial setup of Fallbrook as a 501(c)3 was appropriate. As the school has leaned into business enterprise programs, it has failed to keep up with the requirements for keeping those profit centers separate from the school. Most of the enterprise programs do turn a small profit. Combined, it totals around ten thousand dollars per year. If this money comes from the school's activity, rather than the profit centers, it needs to be reported, which may reduce the funding allocated to the school. When I plugged in this information into the funding allocation programs, the difference in funding was negligible, but did impact distribution for after-school programs."

"So, why do they make such a big deal about it?" Katie grumbled.

"Sometimes the appearance of things is more important that the reality," Irene explained. "Fallbrook needs to go out of its way to avoid any impression that they are improperly enriching themselves."

Katie huffed.

Irene let the silence hang for a moment. "Another finding will be that the FYS program should be revamped or discontinued. I could not find any evidence of wrongdoing or improper procedure; however, the board will be warned that certain actions do not enhance the fiscal credibility of the school. When boiled down to the essentials, the program pays the kids to do their homework with the lure of a fancy trip."

Katie looked frustrated. "It is a good program. What do you want us to do to get through to these children? Beat them?"

Irene shook her head. "No, not that. What I wanted to do was encourage you to find a financial manager who specializes in school funding. An audit is not sufficient. Find someone who is fluent with school funding and who can help you craft the program specifications to smooth over the rough edges. If the funding path was clearer, I think the program could be viewed as an asset instead of a bribe."

Katie frowned. "This is a great deal of money you are asking us to spend. A specialized accountant, another office staffer for 'separation of duties'."

Irene nodded. "These are suggestions. My report will outline them, but the overall conclusion will be that Fallbrook is acting within the laws of Oregon. It will be up to the board if they want to implement the suggestions."

\*\*\*\*

Next, Irene met with Gene Schuster who looked unusually harried. "Can you explain why the kids dial up their creative troublemaking setting on days when I'm most busy?"

Irene smiled. "When I'm in the office working on a deadline, the phone never stops ringing. If I have a light day, it's quiet as the grave."

He grunted. "Does this meeting mean we are almost done?"

"It does, but I need cover some things with you before I can get out of your hair."

He grunted again.

"I met with Katie and went over my findings. My report will say that the school is in the clear, but there are a variety of issues that could stand some improvement."

He frowned. "What? Why?"

"I gave Katie a list of things. I think the board needs to hire a couple of additional positions. An accountant who specializes in schools and another office person to help with ordering, not in the least to get some of that off your shoulders."

He looked annoyed. "We don't have the budget for

that."

Irene studied him for a moment. "Gene, in the last five years, the school has reimbursed you over fifty-five thousand for various purchases. That is an astronomical amount. *Ast-Tro-Nom-I-Cal.* While I can't find any sign that all the purchases and reimbursements were not justified, the mere fact that you are acting as a *de facto* banker for the school raises a great deal of concern. The paperwork alone must be astronomical, and if I were on the board, I'd be worried that you are going into debt while waiting for reimbursements."

Irene saw a quick dart of his eyes to the right. She frowned. "The state has contracting laws that I'm sure you're aware of. It's easier to hire someone to keep you aboveboard than it is to go through an even more stringent audit in a few years when someone else complains."

"The process takes so long."

"I agree. I work for the state, so I do know. But sometimes the appearance of things is more important than the reality. The situation with Phyllis is an example of that. Many mistakes and miscommunications happened with her employment. While she wasn't justified in her accusations, I think she had a right to question how some of these decisions were being made.

"My report will make clear that her concerns are unfounded. She may choose to continue her wrongful termination suit, but I encourage you to let the board handle that. The fact of her accusations means Fallbrook's staff and board will have to work to overcome them."

He indicated his understanding.

"The final thing," Irene said, checking a final item

off the list in front of her, "is a personal suggestion."

He looked startled. "Personal?"

"Yes. I've been impressed with the school. I think you are doing something wonderful here. And, I want to encourage you, personally, to start delegating some duties.

"The other day a friend pointed out that I didn't have to do everything myself. It got me to thinking. I spoke to Darrel Berg, your former board member, this morning. He told me that you didn't appear to trust his offers of help."

She studied Schuster for a moment before continuing. "Allowing people to help is more time-consuming and frustrating. But when you do everything, you become a lightning rod for criticism." She paused. "This school and these children need you. Don't let yourself get burned-out. Ask for help."

Irene stood up and offered her hand. Gene shook it. "Thank you. Even under the circumstances, it's been nice to meet you."

"Thank you." He hesitated. "I'll think about what you said. I can't promise, but lately I've been questioning if the school can go on. I've been teaching for thirty-four years, the last eight as principal of this school. Retirement is starting to sound good."

"Succession planning is one of the hallmarks of a good leader. I hope you'll consider it your next job to train the next principal."

****

Irene arrived at the humane society to pick up the dog. He came out, tail wagging, head in a cone, confused and glum. When he saw her, his expression changed to ecstatic, and he hit the end of the leash so hard the vet

185

tech stumbled. Irene held out her arms but was thoroughly assaulted by the cone and tail. She grabbed for his leash and got him out the door.

Once outside, he promptly lifted his leg. Irene praised him, then loaded him into the car. She heard his tail banging against the side of the crate. "You're a silly goose," she told him.

Chapter 16

Saturday morning, Irene was awakened by the dog's cone banging against the side of the crate. She'd taken it off him for a few hours, but when he began licking his incisions, back on it went.

She glanced at the clock and saw it was a few minutes before the alarm. She got up and took him outside. Already used to the routine, he went to the fence and tried to lift his leg. When that proved painful, he adjusted his stance and returned, running to his food bowl in expectation.

Because she thought giving the dog some exercise before meeting his potential adopter would be wise, she loaded him into his kennel and drove to the park. He sat upright in his kennel as usual, excited about the prospect of going anywhere. At the north parking lot, they unloaded and merged into the steady stream of park goers. The dog contentedly trotted along, smelling all the smells. Irene smiled at how far he had come in two weeks.

Was she really going to give him up? Having him felt like a piece of her life had returned. She was eager to get up in the morning for their walk and happy to get home and see him. She daydreamed of taking him to agility classes. On the other hand, her recent MS flare-up was a serious warning. The sudden increase in exercise coupled with skipping Tuesday and Thursday yoga classes reminded her she couldn't afford to be careless.

They were returning to her car when the phone rang. She pulled it out of her pocket. It was Angie. "Hey."

"Hey," Angie returned, sounding listless.

"How are you?" Irene asked.

"Wiped out. That's why I'm calling. Can you take the boys today? I need a break."

Irene thought about it. "I am meeting a potential adopter for my foster dog—"

"What foster dog?" Angie asked.

"The gray dog. You met him the other day. Remember?"

"I thought that was your new dog. You didn't tell me he was a foster."

Irene decided not to argue. "Anyway. I'm meeting a potential adopter at eleven. But after that, I could take the boys. Do you want me to come get them?"

"That would be perfect. I can take them to soccer and then meet you at the Funplex for the handover. You can bring them back this evening."

"Sounds good. Have they been wanting to go to the Funplex?"

"They always want to go to the Funplex."

"Do you have an objection if we try something else?" Irene asked.

****

Irene arrived at the shelter and went in to say hello to the staff. They confirmed that the potential adopter, Neal, hadn't arrived yet. Irene returned to her car and took the dog out, wanting him to have a chance to sniff and relieve himself before meeting a new friend.

A few minutes later, a gray sedan pulled into the

parking lot, and an older gentleman got out of the car. He was followed by two boys around her nephews' age.

He waved at Irene and the gray dog. "Are you Irene?"

Irene waved back. "Yes. And this is Max." The name felt strange to her.

"I decided to bring my grandsons so they could get a chance to meet him, too. My son will be along in a few minutes. He often walks the dogs for us."

"Oh," Irene said.

He marched across the parking lot trailed by his grandchildren. The dog looked interested in the new set of visitors. Irene concentrated on keeping him on a loose leash. Neal was almost within range when he stopped and squatted down to let the dog take a good sniff. The dog relaxed and moved forward to investigate. Soon, Neal and his grandchildren were petting Max. He attempted to roll over onto his back for a belly rub, but he couldn't figure out how to adjust his cone and ended up doing a rather convoluted flop. Everyone laughed.

"He seems like a good dog," said Neal, stroking the dog's ears. "Why do you think he's here?"

Irene recounted her capture of the dog.

"So, they don't know his history. Any signs of abuse?"

Irene shook her head. "No. He's accepted all the training and grooming I've offered. My guess is that he's young and untrained and either escaped from a yard or someone set him loose because he was too much for them."

Neal grunted. "But he's not house-trained."

"Well, as I said, I haven't had a problem with him, but I've been keeping him under strict supervision."

He reached for the leash. "Do you mind if I walk him around?"

Irene hesitated. Foster volunteers weren't supposed to hand over the leash, but it felt churlish to be a stickler for the rules so near the shelter. And the area was enclosed. She handed over the lead.

Neal started off around the yard, and Max followed, shooting Irene worried glances as they got further away. This lasted for a few more yards before the dog sat down and refused to move.

"Ha. I guess he doesn't want to leave you," Neal commented, returning to Max who lunged back in her direction.

"I wouldn't worry about it," Irene said. "I've only had him two weeks. He can't be that attached to me."

Before he could respond, a flock of geese flew low over the yard. The dog's face took on a predatory glee. One of the children started to run ahead of the dog. Refocusing his predator instinct, the dog launched himself toward the child. A big dog came out of the shelter and began barking. Startled, Neal released the leash.

Free, the dog launched himself toward the boy's legs, determined to corral this frisky sheep. The dog crashed into the boy, knocking him off-balance. The boy tried to steady himself by holding onto the dog, but sore from the previous day's surgery, the dog yelped and bared his teeth at the child. The boy promptly started crying.

Irene intervened, grabbing the dog's leash and leading him to the oppose side of the yard.

Neal crouched in front of his grandson and checked him for injuries. "You're okay," he said to the boy who was already hiccupping himself into silence. He turned to Irene. "I see what you mean about him being a lot of dog."

Irene smiled. She hadn't been sure he'd been listening. "He's going to need someone willing to give him large amounts of exercise and training."

Neal nodded. "I like him. He reminds me of a dog I had when I was a kid. I told you. But I don't think he's right for me right now. I guess I hadn't thought through all the various factors, like the grandchildren and the housetraining and the exercise."

"It's good that you realize that now instead of after you brought him home."

"I'd still like to get another dog," Neal explained.

"Let me put him back in my car and let's go talk to the shelter staff."

Marion County had a Facebook group for foster parents. Caretakers could share pictures and insights about their charges. After her conversation with Neal, a brown chihuahua mix had moved into a foster home. Irene had thought the dog would be a good match for Neal. She showed Neal his picture and left him talking to the foster staff, who had in turn already called the dog's foster parent. She was on her way.

Irene returned to her car and sat there for a few minutes, contemplating the turn of events. The dog eyed her in his kennel, clearly hopeful more adventures were coming. The cone banged against the side of the crate as though it had a mind of its own.

A few minutes later, Irene saw a woman emerge from a car with the little chihuahua mix. They must live close by, Irene mused. Moments later, Neal and his grandsons trooped behind the pair to the yard. Irene watched for a few moments. The scene looked like love at first sight.

Irene returned to the lobby. Ashley saw her and came over. "No dice this time," she said sympathetically.

"I didn't think it was a good fit, even over the phone," Irene admitted. "It went better than I thought it would, but he realized that a big, rambunctious dog like this one wouldn't be entirely safe around small children."

Ashley gestured her agreement. "We always ask about children, but in situations like this, with an extended family, you never know who's going to be around the dog."

"Ashley," Irene took a deep breath. "I think I'd like to adopt him."

A huge smile broke out on her face. "I was wondering what was taking so long."

The front door opened again, and Neal reentered, carrying the chihuahua mix. "I want to adopt him," he announced.

****

Irene explained to Ashley about needing to pick up her nephews. They agreed to meet in a couple of days to finish the paperwork.

With Goose in the car, she drove to her nephews' soccer practice. Dave had turned ten and was enjoying fourth grade, though sports was his real avocation. Mike, in first grade, was content to read and play with toys. Both boys, however, loved anything having to do with large vehicles, particularly trucks with large tires. Irene had noticed that the monster truck rally was happening Saturday at the state fairgrounds. She meant to ask Angie if she could take the boys but hadn't got around to it.

Irene told the boys where they were going, but that they needed to drop Goose off first.

"Goose," they cried in unison.

"Yes, Goose. Because he's a silly goose." And because geese were part of both events that brought us together. "We'll call him loosey Goosey." The boys giggled and chattered at him through the crate door. His tail banged.

"Why does he have to wear that thing?" asked Mike.

"He had a surgery a few days ago. If he doesn't wear it, he'll scratch and get it all infected."

"Like chicken pox," Mike said solemnly.

"Are you really going to keep him?" Dave asked.

"Yeap."

"Is he going to be like Percy?"

"That's the plan."

He pondered that for a while. "Does Mule like him?"

Though she didn't understand where the question was going, Irene answered, "So far, they get along. They've played together at the park a couple of times."

"I like Mule," Dave said.

They returned to Irene's house, had lunch, and played with Goose. Irene settled him into his crate, then they left for the fairgrounds. Irene enjoyed walking the few blocks with the boys because of their never-ending stream of observations and questions.

"That house is pink."

"Do you know that lady?"

"Why is there a stuffed dog in that person's yard?"

"That car isn't parked on the driveway."

"Do you like Spiderman or Wonder Woman better?"

Once at the fairgrounds, Irene purchased entry

tickets, and they spent some time examining the various cars. She did her best to admire the enormous wheels, fancy paint jobs, and potential for "crushing" the other cars.

This wasn't her first child-oriented outing. After an hour they sat on a bench, enjoying snacks, then a drink, then a trip to the bathroom. Not so different than dogs, Irene mused, watching her nephews walk together to the men's room.

Her plan was to stay until the boys got tired, go home for dinner, then return for the evening show. The boys had their own set of pajamas and various other items at the house. Irene would deliver the boys back to Angie at church the next morning.

They had finished dinner and were planning to walk back to the fairgrounds for the evening show. Irene was helping Mike put on his jacket when she noticed he looked flushed, and his breathing was audible. "Are you okay, buddy?" she asked.

"My tongue feels funny," he said crankily.

Irene examined him and then picked up the phone to call her sister. "Angie, is Mike allergic to anything?"

"Not that I know of. Why?"

"He's flushed and breathing hard and says his tongue feels funny."

"What did you guys have to eat?"

"Thai. They had the pad Thai, and we had mangoes and sticky rice for dessert."

Angie thought for a moment. "Jason sometimes has a mild reaction to mango. When we were first dating, he ate some and ended up getting a rash."

"Okay. I'm going to take him to the emergency room."

"I'll meet you there."

Irene hung up. "Okay, guys, change of plans. We need to head to the hospital." Irene rushed into the bathroom and grabbed a packet of antihistamine. "Mike, swallow one of these."

In ten minutes, they were at the emergency room. Irene pulled up to the emergency drive-in area and explained the situation to the waiting nurse. The nurse examined Mike and wheeled him in. Irene parked the car and gathered up Dave so they could go inside.

"Sorry about this, buddy," Irene said.

"Will he be okay?" said Dave. He was holding her hand, an unusual event. Dave took his role as the oldest seriously.

"I think so. They'll give him a shot. It should help. If you want, you can ask the doctor when he comes out."

Irene went to the front desk. They handed her a stack of forms, and she went to sit down with Dave. Dave took out his pocket video game. A few moments later, a nurse came out to ask more questions. Irene answered, and the nurse left.

Ten minutes later, Angie came into the waiting room. Dave hugged her and Irene reported what she knew. Angie went to the desk to ask if she could see him, they gave her his room number.

"You wait here," she said. "I'll be right back."

Dave returned to his game. Then he said, "They're getting a divorce, you know. Mom and Dad."

Irene looked over at him. "It sounds that way."

"I don't want Mike to die, too."

"He won't die."

"A kid in my class did. He got stung by a bee."

Irene nodded. "This is different. We got Mike to the

hospital. He'll be okay."

Dave shifted back to marriage. "Why are they getting a divorce?"

"It's complicated."

He gave her an all-too-adult look. "That's what Mom and Dad say, too."

"Right. I don't know why they are getting a divorce. But you know it doesn't have anything to do with you, right?"

He rolled his eyes. "They tell all the kids whose parents get divorces that. Mom already sent me to see the school counselor."

"Sorry," Irene said. "I didn't mean to repeat anything."

"It doesn't make sense that it doesn't have anything to do with me or Mike, though. Dad was always complaining about having to take care of us while Mom was at work. It must have to do with us."

"Do you ever have days where you don't want to go to school?"

"Duh."

"Right. But what would you do if you didn't have to go to school?"

"Play video games."

"Forever? What would you do when you got to be an adult? Would you be happy living with your mom, only playing video games?"

He pondered that. "I don't know."

"Right. So, the issue isn't that you don't want to go to school, the issue is there is something more fun you could do. But if you do the fun thing long enough, you'll get bored. Your dad is kind of saying the same thing. He doesn't want to stay home, even though he loves you and

Mike. He wants to go do more exciting things."

Again, Mike thought. "I guess being an adult is rough."

"Tell me about it."

Chapter 17

Irene felt a sense of *déjà vu* when her brother-in-law knocked on her front door. "Hi, Jason."

"Hey, Irene."

She didn't invite him inside. "I'm about to leave for work."

"I wanted to come by and say thank you for taking care of Mike on Saturday."

"Of course. He's my nephew."

He looked at the ground. Time clicked by.

"Jason, I'm in a hurry."

He ducked his head. "So, you know that Angie and I broke up."

The juvenile term almost amused her. "I know."

"And I quit my job at the dealership."

"I know."

"I'm going back to Alaska."

"I heard."

His shoulders sagged. "I never meant to mess everything up this bad."

"I'm sure you didn't."

"Angie's pretty mad."

"You cheated on her, refused to support her career, and demanded she move back to a place she only tolerated for your sake. I think anger is an appropriate emotion."

"I don't want to lose touch with the boys."

In spite of herself, Irene felt sympathy. "I'm sure Angie would welcome any support you could provide. When you leave the area, set up a phone schedule and stick to it."

He bowed his head again. The silence dragged on. Impatiently, she looked at her watch.

"It's just—" Jason began. "You're always so sure of everything. You know things. I… I'm not sure I want to go."

Irene gazed at him with exasperation. "I think we need to get something straight. I'm Angie's sister. I'm on her side. If you don't know what you want, I sure as hell don't know."

And she shut the door.

****

Irene's office was buzzing with excitement. The interviews for the temporary position she and John had discussed were scheduled throughout the day. As predicted, Cara Berger had put in an application as had Peter Hampton. Peter was visibly nervous. Irene was relieved she wasn't going to be on the interview panel.

Irene went to Peter's desk. "You want to walk over and get a coffee?"

He looked at her in surprise. "I thought you had interviews today."

"I'm not on this panel."

"Oh." He got up and they walked to the next building for coffee.

"Are you ready for the interview?" Irene prodded.

"Yeah. But I think Cara will get it."

Irene agreed. "It wouldn't surprise me. I told John that I think you're ready to be a team lead. Consider this an interview for that. You're ready for a step up, but not this particular one."

He gazed at her. "Do you ever think I'll be ready?"

Irene shrugged. "You can do the work, Peter. It's the politics that give you trouble. I think being a team lead would be a gentle introduction to that."

He acknowledged her words. "Sometimes, I don't know that I'll ever be able to be a leader."

Irene smiled. "You will. But even if you don't, you do your best."

Peter smiled. "Thanks. I needed to hear that."

"Everyone needs to hear that."

****

Phyllis Dixon arrived exactly at her appointed time. Irene had the receptionist escort her to a small conference room. Irene let her sit there for ten minutes before entering. Phyllis looked uneasy and defensive.

"Please forgive me. I had to go over some information. Did anyone offer you coffee? Or water?"

Phyllis shook her head. "I don't need anything."

"Okay. Well, then, let's get started."

"In our previous interview, you stated you had nothing to do with the reporting of registration or deregistration of students. Is that still your position?"

Irene saw a flicker of nerves cross Phyllis's face. "Yes. That was the registrar's job."

"But you were aware that enrollment numbers affected the revenue coming into the school?"

"Of course."

Irene opened a folder. "Are you familiar with this report?" she asked, sliding the paper across the table.

Phyllis took the document and looked it over. "Yes. This is the monthly enrollment report."

"Which was sent to county education department

along with an invoice, prepared by you, requesting payment."

Phyllis agreed again.

Irene took another paper from the folder and gave it to her. "This is also the monthly enrollment report. What do you see?"

Phyllis studied the two reports. They were on identical forms, and each claimed to report for the same period. But the student numbers were not the same. "One of these is obviously incorrect," she replied, folding her hands in her lap.

"Which one?"

"How would I know that?" Phyllis snapped. "That's Chick's job."

"Oh," Irene exhaled. "I thought you'd know because one of these is what Ms. Roy approved, and the other was adjusted by you."

"No."

"Yes. We were able to find the original reports through email exchanged between Ms. Roy and Mr. Schuster. After both parties had signed off, they would put the report on the server. You were then responsible for creating the invoice."

"Which I did."

"You did. Except, you created a shadow enrollment system and used it to track the students, especially the ones on the ESL track."

"No, I didn't."

Irene shook her head sadly. "Both Mr. Schuster and Ms. Roy told me about the arguments you had with them about requesting additional money for the ESL students. They wanted to report conservatively to avoid the perception of double-billing with another grant the school held for the ESL program."

Phyllis's jaw was set, but she didn't respond.

"You said that it wasn't double-billing. The state simply offered the higher amount as a matter of course." Irene paused. "Which, technically, was correct. However, they were unmoved. So, you started changing the reports."

Phyllis scoffed. "How could I do that? They had already signed them."

"That had me stumped for a while," Irene admitted, removing another paper from the stack. The paper was a screenshot of the report within an imaging program. "Both were using digital signature programs that disallowed changes after signing. County education staffers confirmed that you always provided a hard copy request for payment. None of them can find an electronic report. They didn't think anything of it. We took a look, though, and found it was the only report you didn't send electronically.

"I had one of my junior investigators look at it. He thinks you created a duplicate report, then superimposed that report on top of the original report. Programs are sophisticated these days. By the time you printed it off and made a copy, it would be undetectable."

"No. I did not."

Pursing her lips, Irene handed more papers to Phyllis. "These are screen shots of the properties of each document. As you can see, they report the time of creation, creator, and program name. Each of the documents we found on the server listed you as the creator, on a date after Mr. Schuster and Ms. Roy approved the report, with the documents created in a paint program."

Phyllis remained silent.

Irene continued conversationally. "It must have been a tough choice. Should you overwrite the original records, in case Mr. Schuster and Ms. Roy needed to check something? Or should you leave them alone and place your doctored copies where only you could see them?"

Phyllis licked her lips nervously.

"I don't think you were doing it so you could personally make money," Irene tried to keep her voice light. "I think you wanted to bring in the extra money for the school. And to prove Mr. Schuster wrong."

Phyllis's eyes flashed.

"That killed you, didn't it?" Irene said, unable to keep the disdain from her voice. "That you were right, but he didn't have to listen to you. He could do anything he wanted, and you couldn't do a thing about it."

Phyllis looked ready to explode but pulled herself back.

"Probably for the best," Irene complimented, egging her on. "Don't incriminate yourself."

"I did not do anything wrong," Phyllis said, her thin lips barely moving.

"You committed forgery," Irene disagreed.

"The school was entitled to that money."

"Doesn't matter. You submitted forged documents."

Phyllis glared. Irene met her gaze without expression. After a moment, Irene could see Phyllis was starting to think about her predicament.

"It's that asshole, Gene. God, I hate him. He thinks he can do whatever he wants, and everyone on that board worships him." She began crying, reaching into her handbag to find a tissue.

Irene got up and grabbed a box of tissues from the sideboard and put it in front of her.

A few moments passed where the only sound was her sobbing.

Making an attempt to compose herself, Phyllis asked, "Where does this leave me?"

Irene frowned. "Mr. Schuster has spoken to Ms. Roy and his board about this information. Their feeling is that you didn't intend to defraud the school or the county. But they are still facing your wrongful termination suit, our investigation, and an audit by the education department. They would like you to drop your suit and write a letter of apology, confessing to your actions. In exchange, they will not pursue the forgery or fraud charges."

"It wasn't fraud," Phyllis said hotly. "I was trying to get the school what they were owed."

Irene studied her. "We've done our due diligence to investigate your allegations. While my report won't be ready for a few weeks, I will tell you that I have found no evidence of wrongdoing on the part of the school. My report will recommend some process changes, but there will be no major findings."

Phyllis's eyes dried with new anger. "They aren't following proper procedures."

Irene shook her head. "We found nothing to indicate the school is breaking any laws."

"Why are you on their side?"

"I investigate fraud for a living. Almost every person I interviewed on this case impressed me with their earnestness, energy, and responsibility. Except you."

"But I was the only responsible one at that school!"

Irene corrected her. "You had an axe to grind. You shouldn't be working in a school. Drop the charges, write the note, and move on with your life." Irene paused for emphasis. "I think that's the best justice we'll get in this case."

Phyllis looked down at her bag, still using a tissue around her eyes. "I can't promise anything. I need to think about it."

Irene stood up. "I understand. I'll hear about your decision one way or another."

\*\*\*\*

Irene typed the last few words of the Fallbrook report.

Phyllis Dixon announced that she would be dropping her wrongful termination suit. Katie Maldonado called with the news that the board had held a meeting about Irene's recommendations. No decisions had been made yet.

Gene Schuster had contacted Irene privately. He thanked her and asked for recommendations on management consultants that could help him improve his delegation skills.

Cara had been promoted to Criminal Financial Investigator. Peter would move into a team lead role. Peter took it well.

A few weeks later, Candace announced she had found a position closer to her home and would be leaving the division. She confessed to Irene that the work was more to her taste, being standard accounting audits rather than forensic investigations.

\*\*\*\*

Irene went to Sharon's yoga class and then out to dinner with her friend.

"How's Goose doing?" Sharon asked.

"He's doing great. I've enrolled him in a basics class

that will start next week."

"How are you holding up with the exercise portion?"

Irene confessed, "I took your advice and hired a dog walker. She comes in the afternoon. I still try to get him out in the morning and evening."

"Exercise is good for you. But you have to balance it."

"Yes," Irene regarded her plate moodily. "But I still feel guilty."

Sharon reached over and touched Angie's hand. "It takes a village."

Irene squeezed her hand. "Yes."

"How are Angie and the kids doing with the move? Without Jason?"

"I'm not sure. Things are moving quickly. Angie's already got a house located in Bend and wants to move over spring break."

"That's fast."

"Yeah."

"How's your mom doing with it all?"

"With her usual aplomb. She hates Jason and will miss the boys."

Sharon laughed, knowing Jennifer never took anything "with aplomb". "How do you feel about having Angie and the boys so far away?"

Irene forked up a bite of her salad and pondered. "I'll miss having her and the kids nearby and having them pop over on the weekends. We'll phone and email. Add the occasional video conference session and a monthly visit." She smiled. "But I am looking forward to knowing they can't descend at a moment's notice."

"Boundaries," Sharon intoned. "Finally."

"Maybe." Irene gave Sharon a wicked smile. "Jennifer met Goose."

"Oh my God, what happened?"

"She dropped by one afternoon and let herself into the house to wait for me to come home. Goose was out in the mudroom, and she heard him. She opened the door, like she would have done if it was Percy."

"Oh, no."

"Oh, yes. He bounced out, jumped on her, pushed her over, and proceeded to pin her by licking her face for the next few minutes. When I got home, she had put him outside again and was practically in hysterics. I let Goose back in and tried to get her to work with him on a sit, but she wouldn't do it. When I told her to 'treat' she'd throw the cookie at him, which would get him wound up again. She left a few minutes later."

Sharon laughed.

****

Irene, Jennifer, Angie, and the boys sat together in church for the last time. After lunch, Angie and the boys would drive over to Bend. Jennifer had decided to go over to help with the move. Both boys were keyed up and anxious for the appointed time to arrive. Finally, Angie set Mike between Jennifer and Irene and took Dave onto her lap.

By some miracle, the group made it to the end of service and went to a new Chinese restaurant that Jennifer wanted to try. Irene's heart dropped when they entered the restaurant. The décor was polished silver and gold, which appealed to Jennifer, but underwhelmed the boys. Even more alarming was the menu. It was set in Chinese characters with English translations below, and the dishes were not familiar to any of them. Irene looked for something simple.

Sensing the chances for embarrassment were high, the boys immediately turned into budding gourmands. Normally, when they ordered at Chinese restaurant, the boys had turned up their noses and ordered noodles. Today, they wanted the entire menu read to them and made faces at things that didn't suit their fancy.

The server came and more difficulties commenced. This authentic Chinese restaurant had an authentic Chinese server. She bobbed her head pleasantly but couldn't answer any of their questions about how things were prepared or their spice level. Irene ordered chicken and vegetables in a spicy sauce over rice. Jennifer ordered a vegetable concoction. Angie ordered noodles for Dave, the pork dish Mike insisted on trying, and a beef and rice dish for herself. She gave them their video games while they waited and played quietly.

"I wanted to thank both of you for your support in this," Angie said. "You've been wonderful."

"That's what family is for," Irene said. "To lift heavy boxes and supply the booze."

Angie laughed.

"That Jason," Jennifer grumbled.

Angie shook her head. "Not in front of the boys, Jennifer."

Jennifer looked like she wanted to argue but decided against it.

"Will you try to sleep in the house tonight?" Irene asked.

Angie shook her head. "No, we'll be in a motel tonight. The movers are driving over today, and we set up a color-coded system so they can unpack various things into each room. Tomorrow we'll go to the house.

I've arranged for the company to come back for a few hours to help us move anything heavy into position."

"That sounds good," Irene approved. "Do I dare ask when I might rate an invitation?"

Angie smiled. "Whenever you want."

Jennifer began to talk about some interesting real estate customers, then Angie imparted some funny stories about car buyers. Irene related the Fallbrook case.

"So, what happened?" asked Jennifer, forking up a vegetable. In spite of the rough start, the food was good. "Did she drop the lawsuit?"

Irene inclined her head. "Yep."

"Jason called me the other night," Angie announced. Jennifer and Irene stopped eating to look at her.

"He called you? Or, like, he called the house to talk to the boys and spoke to you?" Irene asked cautiously.

"He called *me*," she repeated. "He said he just wanted to hear the sound of my voice."

Jennifer and Irene looked at each other.

"He says that Alaska is colder than he remembers. He's excited he got onto a North Slope oil crew. He asked if he could come visit us and stay at the new house next month."

"What did you say?" Jennifer asked.

"I told him that the new house had an extra bedroom that would be available for him."

"That's reasonable."

"I miss him," Angie confessed. "And I know he misses me. But we can't go back."

"You don't have to decide today. Get settled. Then you might be ready to think about that."

Angie reached out and took their hands. "I'll miss you two being close."

All three women sniffled.

The boys looked up from their games and made gagging faces. "Tears. Only girls cry."

"We are girls," Jennifer said tartly. In disgust, the boys went back to their games.

\*\*\*\*

That evening, Irene sat watching television, idly caressing Goose. Her mind wasn't on the program. Gary had texted her this afternoon to remind her of his invitation to the dog show next weekend.

An hour later, she took Goose out for his final walk of the evening. As they walked, she heard the cry of geese finding their final evening roost.

Her hand drifted to her pocket. She opened her phone, scrolled to Gary's text, and typed "*Yes*".

## A word about the author…

Tara Choate writes from her home base of Lincoln City, Oregon. A native Oregonian, she has had a varied career around the state.

Tara is supervised by her rescue dog, Key, and two cats, Chitza and Anouk. Since getting her first dog, she has enjoyed competing with her dogs in dog agility, but shifted her focus to canine nose work as age caught up with her.

Tara is also a watercolor artist. You can view a gallery of Tara's works, upcoming events, works in progress, and upcoming titles at www.tarachoate.com.

Thank you for purchasing
this publication of The Wild Rose Press, Inc.

For questions or more information
contact us at
info@thewildrosepress.com.

The Wild Rose Press, Inc.
www.thewildrosepress.com

www.ingramcontent.com/pod-product-compliance
Lightning Source LLC
Chambersburg PA
CBHW051649260626
47170CB00004B/1407